SHELTER FROM THE STORM

PORT PROVIDENT: HURRICANE HOPE
BOOK ONE

KRISTEN ETHRIDGE

To Mrs. Wilson —
Thank you for a great year and for everything you do for Carrie! Have a great summer!

LAUREL LOCK PUBLISHING

CONTENTS

A GIFT FOR YOU

Dear Reader,

There's a storm coming—and her name is Hope. I know that sounds a little crazy, that something so destructive could be labeled with such a peaceful name. But hope is one of the most powerful forces in the universe. It's even bigger than the storms life throws at us.

I'm glad we're riding out Hurricane Hope together in Port Provident here in *Shelter from the Storm*. I can't wait to introduce you to Ross and Becca (and Cookie and Polly). As Hurricane Hope rolls ashore, it wipes away the familiar structures in Port Provident, but it also breaks down the long-standing barriers between rivals Ross and Becca.

In short, it brings hope for a different future going forward. And that's what Port Provident is all about.

Port Provident is a place to belong, and each sweet escape romance story I write is full of hope, heart, and happily-ever-after. My reader community is built on these ideas as well. I think there's enough discouragement in the world today. When I pick up a book, I want a few hours to myself and a story I can get lost in. I want stories that lift me up and make me smile. And that's why I created Port Provident—a town for all of us to visit for a sweet escape.

I'd like to invite you to join that reader community today. Just go to https://www.subscribepage.com/kristenethridgenewsletter. It's that easy!

I'll send you a free copy of Layla and Ridge's story, *A Place to Find Love,* just for joining my reader community. It's available only to newsletter subscribers, plus you'll be able to keep up with the latest on my books and Port Provident. You may be new to Port Provident, but so is Layla Watson. As she gets to know the town and why it's so special, I think you'll find your own sweet escape in Port Provident too.

I promise these books will leave you with a smile.

All the best,

Kristen

P.S… One of the best ways to get to know Port Provident even better is to get your *Passport to Port Provident.* It's a behind-the-scenes reader exclusive that's available when you join me on Facebook Messenger at
www.facebook.com/kristenethridgebooks

www.kristenethridge.com
www.facebook.com/kristenethridgebooks
www.instagram.com/kristenethridge

1

Ten years ago, Becca Collins caught a bus to Port Provident, Texas because it was as far south as she could get from Wisconsin without falling into the water. She never expected to take another bus to leave.

But today, she found herself standing in a line in front of Port Provident High School, waiting to board a school bus headed for San Antonio. Hurricane Hope was expected to make landfall overnight. This was the last evacuation bus scheduled to cross the Causeway which connected Provident Island with the Texas mainland.

The line had been moving consistently, but now there had been no progress in getting aboard the bus for a few minutes. The crowd, mostly made up of women and children, was beginning to get restless. Becca could hear it in the rustle of voices that were starting to rise above a whisper and in the stirring and stomping of feet as they adjusted the positions where they stood.

She could also feel it in the dense layer of humidity that had pushed ashore with the first bands of Hope's clouds and winds.

Damp circles were beginning to soak through the thin cotton of her T-shirt, and she felt a sticky clamminess working its way down her spine. She just wanted to get on the rattley yellow school bus and get moving. As the director of the Port Provident Animal Shelter, she'd seen the last dog in her care off the island this morning, headed to a shelter in a northern suburb of Houston. The final group of cats had departed around dinner time yesterday. The animals who had depended upon her would be safe.

The only thing left was to ensure her own safety before the storm arrived. If her compact Toyota hatchback wasn't on its last leg, she would have just taken matters into her own hands. But most days, she wasn't sure it would make it to the grocery store. A two-hundred-and-fifty-mile trip that was expected to take double the normal amount of time due to heavy traffic congestion? That was out of the question.

In fact, Becca realized, she might have had a breakdown before the little hatchback. The last few weeks had been so stressful. First the showdown at the board meeting with the president—and most unreasonable member—of the shelter's board of directors, Dr. Ross Reeder. Now Hurricane Hope.

She needed a break, and she needed it now.

She also needed to get on the bus. *What was taking so long?* Becca made a step to the right side of the line, trying to discern the cause of the hold-up.

"I'm sorry. The dog has to stay. We cannot take dogs on the bus or to the shelter." A blonde-haired lady holding a clipboard spoke with a stern voice that carried over the ever-strengthening gusts of wind.

"But she has to come. She's my grandma's dog. She requires a special diet. We can't leave her behind. She'll die." A teenager with a thick black braid down the back of her head spoke up, then gestured at a Labrador retriever near her feet.

"Then she'll have to stay behind with the dog. The Port Provident Animal Shelter is closed. Your only options are to get on board without the dog or to stay here with her. I'm sorry, but we can't make exceptions."

"But Grandma can't stay. She's not in good health. I take care of her." She gave another look down toward the dog's sturdy head. "And, so does Polly. We're all a team."

The woman with the clipboard shifted slightly, blocking a little more of the door to the bus. "I'm sorry. Those are the rules. You need to decide. We have to be loaded and en route in ten minutes and there's a whole line behind you."

A dog. A grandmother. Becca looked heavenward. She took a deep breath as the memories of Bess popped into her head like fragile soap bubbles.

"I'll take the dog." Becca picked up her backpack and slung it over one shoulder, then walked toward the Labrador and her visibly-shaking owner. "I'm Becca Collins, director of the Port Provident Animal Shelter. The shelter is closed. But I'll stay behind with your dog."

The girl turned her head slowly. The older woman's eyes released a stream of silent tears.

"You'll take Polly? But you don't even know us."

"I don't. But I know all about dogs and grandmothers. And hard choices."

Becca held out her hand for the leash. With deliberate, almost hesitant motions, the girl pressed the loop end of the leash into Becca's outstretched palm. Becca felt the worn weave of the purple fabric.

"Wait." The girl said, reaching into a reusable grocery store bag and pulling out a bag of specialized dog food. "There's a prescription label on the bag with directions for how to feed her. Oh, and we have to keep her well-hydrated."

"You said her name was Polly?" Becca said, giving the dog a scratch behind the flopped-over ears.

The grandmother spoke. The syllables cracked like popcorn. "Polly Wolly Doodle. I'll be back for her. Take care of her, please."

"All the day...all the day." Becca scratched the dog's ears again as her own throat tightened. Her own grandmother had loved Shirley Temple movies. As clearly as though it had happened yesterday, Becca remembered pushing a VHS tape in the recorder and snuggling on the couch with Bess, watching Shirley's little curls bounce as she sang Polly Wolly Doodle. "She'll be waiting for you when you come home. You'll find us both at the Port Provident Animal Shelter."

Before Becca knew it, everything was taken care of. Within two minutes of the last resident of Port Provident taking their seat, the bus was out of the parking lot, and the last group of evacuees was on their way off the island. The engine of the bus jumped to life with a diesel-fuel rattle…and then there was nothing but silence.

Becca stood in the parking lot, rooted. The last transport was gone, and she was not. She was still in the parking lot of Port Provident High School. With a dog. And a less than half a bag of expensive prescription-only dog food.

She lifted the bag and looked at the label stuck in the center.

Dr. Ross Reeder.

Of course, Polly's vet was Ross Reeder. Because if there was one person she wanted to stay clear of today—well, every day, really—it was Port Provident's haughty, argumentative vet. The president of the board of directors of the Port Provident Animal Shelter, Ross had blocked Becca's plan to relocate the shelter from the old, outdated facility on Harborview Drive to a building in town that she believed in her heart would give them room to grow.

He'd made every step of the last two months feel like a twenty-mile hike in the mountains. Without shoes. Or a trail.

Dealing with him was painful.

But she'd committed to keeping Polly the Labrador safe and healthy—and she knew the half-empty bag of dog food was not going to last a dog of Polly's size very long. She also knew this specific, specialized brand was only sold in one place on the island.

Dr. Ross Reeder's office.

Ugh. The syllable pushed into every fiber of her body like some kind of green viscous slime. In fact, that feeling summed up her impression of Ross. Everywhere she turned with regard to the new shelter location, every idea she had…there he was, guaranteed to put a suffocating blanket of negativity over it all.

Polly thumped her tail on the ground twice, oblivious to Becca's internal dilemma. The simple canine gesture did remind her though that she'd promised to take care of this furry patient, and one of the basics of care was food.

Besides, most of Port Provident's citizens had already heeded the recommendations to evacuate. Ross Reeder was probably one of them.

He was too uptight and by-the-book to go through a hurricane. He'd probably left before Mayor Blankenship's press conference yesterday that implored residents to leave Provident Island.

Becca didn't know Ross well—and she didn't want to know him well—but clearly, he didn't have an adaptable gene in his body. Becca assumed that staying on the island through a storm like this would take a lot of go-with-the-flow.

So, she'd knock on the door of Dr. Reeder's office, and when he wasn't there, she'd drive back over to the animal shelter and get some of the prescription food they had stocked in the back room. It was a slightly different formula, made by a different company—and a good rule of thumb was not to quickly change a dog's diet, especially a specialized one—but it was also highly recommended for canine kidney patients, and it should work for a few days until everything returned to normal.

She gave one more scratch behind Polly Wolly Doodle's furry ears. "Come on, girl, let's figure out our new game plan."

Polly let out a sound that was more bellow than woof. She hadn't really even expressed wariness at being left with a stranger. She seemed like a kind, trusting dog. You could see it in her tired, old eyes. Becca interpreted the dog's strong vocalization to mean that Polly was ready for what was to come. The idea made her chuckle. Polly the Labrador probably had more go-with-the-flow in her four chunky paws than Ross Reeder had in his whole body.Dr. Ross Reeder pulled the zipper around the perimeter of the suitcase where he'd put the last of the supplies he and his traveling companion would need in the days ahead. It was time to go. He didn't know when the Causeway would be closing, but judging by the strength of the wind, it would not be a viable evacuation route much longer. The Texas Department of Transportation had been very clear in a televised press conference a few hours ago that once winds reached a certain speed, it would be too hazardous for cars to drive across the tall bridge which spanned the more than seven hundred feet that separated Provident Island from the rest of the continental United States.

Ross locked the door on the room where he kept all his veterinary pharmaceuticals and supplies.

"Come on, Cookie. Let's get in the truck." Ross snapped his fingers and headed for the stairs with the attentive cream-colored Labrador retriever who was never far from his heels.

As he walked through the main floor of the house to ensure that everything in the clinic area was as secure as he could make it, Ross noticed he'd left the television on in the front room. Typically, this space served as a waiting room for his patients and their owners, but today—like much of the rest of the island—it was empty. He put his suitcase down and walked over to catch one last glance at Rick O'Connell's report on National Weather News, the country's leading twenty-four-hour weather network.

When Rick O'Connell showed up, that was shorthand for a storm that meant business.

Ross had seen enough excitement for a lifetime. After serving as an Army veterinarian in Iraq—where he'd saved a burned and bloodied Cookie after the furry hero's handler was killed by an IED—Ross was done with drama.

He'd moved to Port Provident a few years ago and wanted nothing other than to practice a more mundane form of veterinary medicine than what the Army offered, punctuated by watching sunrises and sunsets over the Gulf of Mexico from the widow's walk porch that crossed the roof on the back of the hundred-year-old house from which he operated his veterinary clinic.

Cookie was already waiting at the back door which led to the garage at the rear of the lot on which the distinguished Victorian house sat. Ross could hear the muffled thumps of Cookie's thick tail as it popped rhythmically on the hardwood floor.

Then Ross heard another thump from the front of the house—a pounding on the front door.

Who would be coming to a vet clinic in the middle of a hurricane evacuation?

Ross opened the door and couldn't believe what stood on the porch in front of him. One of his favorite patients...and one of his least favorite people.

But...Becca Collins did not own Polly McCaw.

"What are you doing here?" Ross knew his greeting sounded more like an outburst, but he was confused and running out of time. There wasn't really an opportunity for pleasantries. Not that anything was ever pleasant when stubborn, head-in-the-clouds Becca Collins was involved.

"Well hello to you too. I figured you'd be gone by now."

As usual, she made virtually no sense. "So why are you here? And what are you doing with Polly? Where's Eloise McCaw?"

A wind gust freed several strands of hair from the front of Becca's dark ponytail and blew them across her face. She tucked them behind her ear, where they promptly blew askew again. "She's on a bus to San Antonio with her granddaughter. They wouldn't let her take the dog."

"So, someone from the city called the shelter?" Ross kept watching the flutter of the wayward locks of hair.

"I volunteered. I was behind them in line. Polly's owner wouldn't go unless she knew Polly was safe. But she's in bad health and couldn't stay behind with Polly. The shelter is closed. The last dog left the island earlier today, headed up to a shelter in Montgomery County. I was following behind."

"On the public evacuation bus?"

She pursed her lips and nodded briefly. "Yes. We don't all make a doctor's salary. Some of us have to take advantage of other available resources sometimes."

Ross could hear the bitterness in her words. It was like listening to a lemon.

"What do you need from me?" Now he knew how Becca and Polly came to be together. He still wasn't sure, though, why they were on his clinic's porch.

She reached into a bag at her feet and pulled out a folded-up white bag. "Dog food. They didn't leave me with enough kibble, and I'd rather not change Polly's food if I can avoid it since she's on a special diet."

"Dog food? That's it?" This was far less complicated than most of the plans Becca dreamed up. "I've got some in the back. You two can come inside if you'd like."

Becca shrugged, then leaned over and picked up the bag at her feet. "Okay."

Ross held the door open as the pair walked in, then went back to re-open the storage room he'd just locked. When he came back, carrying two bags of Polly's prescription food, he saw Becca standing in front of the television in the waiting room. Her shoulders slumped under the straps of the backpack. Her whole demeanor changed from what it had seemed to be only moments before.

Ross placed the bags at Becca's feet, and Polly gave each a hearty sniff.

"What's wrong?" He asked.

Becca waved a hand at the TV screen. "They just closed the Causeway. We're stuck."

"No, they aren't closing the Causeway until four. TxDoT had a press conference a couple of hours ago. They won't close it until the wind hits a certain speed."

She shook her head and pointed at Rick O'Connell. "It wasn't the wind. It was the storm surge. Provident Bay is rising faster than they expected. The waves and current are proving to be too much for the Causeway. They are saying there may be structural damage below the surface of the water now. It's definitely closed. We're trapped."

Trapped. He thought back to Iraq and one particular ride in a convoy where he felt the eyes of insurgents on the back of his neck at every turn. He'd never felt more trapped in his life—a sitting duck, just waiting for whatever was going to happen. The memory poked at the deepest corners of his stomach, filling his whole body with a sense of unease.

Instantly, his thoughts turned to Cookie. Cookie had seen more and lived through more in Iraq than Ross had—and suffered the effects of it. Staying through a hurricane wasn't an option for Cookie. It would be more stress than Cookie could handle.

"There has to be an option."

"There isn't. Listen to the report. There's the head of the Texas Department of Transportation being interviewed. And that's the mayor standing next to him." She turned and looked Ross straight in the eye. "Do you have to disagree with everything I say?"

"You're picking the wrong fight on the wrong day."

"I'm not picking a fight. I'm reading the crawl at the bottom of the screen—also known as the very clear writing on the wall. It is what it is, whether you like the fact that I'm the one who told you or not." Becca leaned over and shoved one of the food bags in with the half-empty bag she'd been given by the McCaws. She slung the blue carrying bag over her shoulder and picked up the second bag Ross had handed her and tucked it in the crook of her arm. Becca gave the purple leash a tug. "Come on, Polly, let's go. We've got to figure out a plan."

Even loaded down with dog food and Labrador, she still looked like the same stubborn Becca that she was at every single board meeting for the Port Provident Animal Shelter. She carefully reached one hand out as far as she could without toppling her carefully-balanced load and turned the doorknob. The heavy, solid wood door blew back in her face.

Polly jerked off to the side, and Becca lost her footing, tumbling to the floor amid a pile of bags.

"Are you okay?" Ross didn't like her, but he certainly didn't want her hurt. Especially not with a hurricane coming.

"I'm fine." The syllables were short and static. She adjusted the mess around her, propped herself up carefully, then stood.

Ross watched her struggle with rearranging her load and grabbed a bag of dog food and returned it back to its place.

"What's your plan?" he asked.

"My plan?" She cast a glance over her shoulder as she stood in the doorway.

"Yeah, where are you going?" Watching her fall to the floor made Ross realize he needed to set aside his usual opinion of Becca for a few moments. As much as he wished the breaking report on TV wasn't true, the simple fact was that they were both in the same boat now. Stuck on Provident Island. Stuck in the crosshairs of Hurricane Hope.

They weren't stuck together—thankfully, because he knew he couldn't handle that—but he did need to make sure she was going to be okay for at least the hours to come. That was the right thing to do.

It was the honorable thing to do.

He'd been out of the Army for a while, but honor and duty still remained the backbone of who he was. That was true in the dustbox of Iraq, and it was no different here in Port Provident.

The leash pulled tight as Polly kept trotting along while Becca didn't.

"I don't really know," she said, shoulders rounding again. "Plan A was to take the city-organized evacuation bus. So was Plan B. And Plan C. I don't think I can go home."

Her voice had softened, and it made Ross take note. This wasn't the combative Becca he so often encountered.

"Where's home?"

She turned to face him. "A studio apartment at the back of the shelter."

The Port Provident Animal Shelter backed up to one of the marshiest spots on Provident Island. Stuck between Harborview Drive and the harbor itself, there was virtually no doubt that the building would take on water, and probably a lot of it.

"You're right. That's probably not an option."

"I guess they'll open up the high school as a shelter. I'd heard some city officials talking about that as I waited in line. Councilwoman Angela Ruiz was there with her daughter, and she said there would be someplace safe for families to go."

Ross looked past Becca and Polly, to the almost totally deserted curb and street. "Where's your car?"

The rain had picked up significantly just in the few minutes they'd been inside. The curbs in this area of town had been laid during an era where the residents of Port Provident traveled in horses and buggies and carriages and needed a higher edge to step onto.

Ross could clearly see the water puddling over the top of the tall curb—which meant anything on the street was about to flood and be useless.

"I had a spot at the highest point in the parking lot over at the high school, so I left the car there. You weren't too far away, and the rain wasn't too bad, so Polly and I walked. But look at the storm now." She bit her lower lip and twisted it slightly between her teeth. "There goes Plan D. And probably my car. This is getting a little too real, too fast."

"Tell me about it." Ross watched the motion of the gray clouds overhead and the sustained shaking of the branches in the trees. "How about I drive you over there? I've got a truck with four-wheel drive. That should be able to get us through this. The high school isn't too far away."

A small light caught in her eyes. They were a rich velvet brown. Ross had never noticed that before.

"You'd do that for me?"

"For Polly," Ross said, then grinned broadly. "She's one of my favorite patients."In the time that Becca had been gone to Ross' office, another line had formed at Port Provident High School, this time leading up the front steps to the entrance of the school.

The rain slapped against the windshield of Ross' truck, and the wipers beat out a fast tempo, but couldn't wipe away the water fast enough. In the last hour, things had really taken a turn for the worst—a harbinger of things to come. There wasn't just wind and rain in the air, there was a thick shroud of tension. Becca could feel it in every cell of her body.

She hadn't been this nervous about anything in a long time. Certainly not since she left Milwaukee.

Cookie and Polly huddled together on the bench-style seat behind Becca. Canine intuition. The dogs knew something was coming, too.

"You can wait here for a second until the line goes down if you want," Ross offered. "It looks like the line is starting to move faster, but there's no reason to stand outside in this mess."

"I think we'll be okay." Becca reached down toward the floorboard, where she'd placed her backpack and all the dog food. "Thanks again for bringing us over here. Good luck to you, Dr. Reeder."

Becca stuck out her hand, feeling somewhat ridiculous—but not knowing exactly what to do here. She and Dr. Ross Reeder were never on the same side of anything. It felt a little awkward to know they were basically in the same boat right now—figuratively speaking—right down to a companion Labrador retriever for each of them.

Ross took her offered hand. Becca never thought she'd have expectations of a handshake with Ross Reeder, but it definitely took her by surprise that she noticed how smooth his hands were.

"You sure you'll be okay here?" He looked at the door to the high school, then back to Becca.

"Here? Of course. You wouldn't believe what I've seen in my life. A hurricane doesn't scare me." She put one two fingers behind the door latch and tugged, popping the door open. "Well, not that much."

Polly hesitated after Becca got out then opened the back door. She wiggled her big brown nose and sniffed at the rain-soaked air, giving Becca a look of chocolatey wariness.

"Come on, Polly. I'm getting soaked." Becca gave the leash a tug, and Polly pushed up from her seated position and placed one paw slowly in front of the other, then hopped.

Becca closed both doors quickly and gave a quick half-wave back at Ross and Cookie as she headed straight for the open glass door, Polly in tow.

"Stop, ma'am. The dog can't come in here." A police officer stood at the top of the steps and held up his hand.

"Can't come in? This is the shelter of last resort. Where else am I supposed to go?" A feeling like claustrophobia began to crowd in on Becca. She couldn't breathe properly.

"You can go right on in. The dog can't." The police officer didn't even crack a sympathetic smile.

"But she's old, and she has health problems. I can't leave her alone in a hurricane. She could die."

The man shifted slightly, positioning himself more directly between Becca and the door. "I'm very sorry about your dog, ma'am, but those are the rules. For a number of health and safety reasons, animals of any kind are not allowed in the shelter."

Rain started to blow almost sideways, throwing a wall of water directly under the overhang where Becca and Polly were attempting to stay as dry and calm as they possibly could.

It wasn't working.

Nothing was working.

Suddenly, Polly sneezed, coating the back of Becca's leg with a fine sheen of dog-mist. Becca barely noticed.

Becca's heart squeezed. She couldn't let Polly's family down.

She couldn't let Polly down.

Since the minute the worn purple leash had been placed in Becca's hand, Polly had been a trooper. She'd remained calm and had looked up at Becca with deep brownie-colored eyes filled with warm trust. She'd instantly sensed that Becca would help her, would take care of her.

Becca took the trust of dogs seriously.

A loyal basset hound named Rupert had taught her that valuable life lesson almost two decades ago.

She knelt down in front of the creamy-colored dog and put a hand on either side of Polly's face, then leaned down so her forehead touched the wide, flat top of Polly's head. Becca's grandmother, Bess, prayed about everything. But Becca hadn't seen much use in it. Her childhood had shown her that prayers went unanswered.

But maybe just this once…

Her tears mingled with the drops of rain soaking Polly's fur. "Please God, I don't even know what letter we're on anymore, but we need a plan. A real one. One that works for both of us."

A horn honked in the distance. *Beep. Beep. Beep-beep-beeeeeep.*

Becca broke her prayer off and hoped that God wouldn't hold the impatience of some jerk in the parking lot against her. She'd tried to pray a real prayer. It clearly just wasn't meant to be. She hadn't even gotten to say "amen" or any of that stuff you had to do for the prayer to count.

She heard another *beep* and looked up, turning her head toward the sound.

The headlights on Ross Reeder's truck were flashing on and off, then on and off again. As she stared, the truck drove toward the door. Ross rolled down the window.

"What's going on? You need a Plan E? Or is this Plan F? I can't keep track anymore."

Becca looked at Polly, then up at Ross, then back at Polly again. The dog stared soulfully, then pointed her muzzle toward the door of the car and stood.

Becca stood too, wiping her forearm across her cheeks, trying to get rid of the tears that had snuck out.

"I think this might be G," she said.

Ross nodded. "You may be right. At any rate, grab that dog food and let's G-O." He pointed at the clouds in the sky, lined up in gray rows for as far as the eye could see. "I don't think we've got much time to lose."

2

*R*oss drove slowly through the street. Water splashed everywhere—down from the sky, up from the tires, and some from places and directions that he couldn't even begin to identify. He didn't dare take his eyes from the road, but he felt acutely aware of Becca's presence in the passenger seat next to him, even if he couldn't safely turn to see her.

As he focused on getting back home in one piece, his mind wandered slightly. He knew he had to keep his concentration as the streets of Port Provident became increasingly treacherous, but he struggled to wrap his thoughts around the changes which had happened in the last hour.

Sixty minutes ago, he had a suitcase in hand and was ready to get in the truck and drive off the island before the Causeway closed. Then a knock at the door came, and all his careful plans changed.

While he didn't like the idea of being trapped on the island, he'd been in Iraq. He'd seen much worse. And that deployment had lasted for months. Hurricane Hope would be over in probably less than thirty-six hours. He could do anything for thirty-six hours.

He allowed himself the briefest of glances to his right. Well, almost anything.

Ross wasn't sure what was going to happen to him, being in the presence of Becca Collins for thirty-six hours. She usually drove him up the wall in less than thirty-six minutes.

"Do you live near the clinic?" She asked softly, breaking up his thoughts.

"A few feet away. There's a garage apartment in the back of the lot, right next to the alley. I live up there."

"So, we're headed back there?"

Her voice was low, and Ross struggled to hear her words against the competing sounds of rain on the roof, windshield wipers on high, and the spray of water under his tires.

"Yeah. About two more blocks."

She didn't say anything in return.

Visibility was almost non-existent, but Ross could make out a yellow-and-red truck parked in front of the clinic. He slowed even more, the truck barely crawling, so he could better tell what was going on.

There was a small boat in the bed of the truck. Ross looked toward the porch and saw an officer knocking on the door. A few alarm bells went off in his head—this wasn't something he could ignore. He parked his truck behind the red-and-yellow one and noticed that the tailgate read "Port Provident Beach Patrol."

No easy way to do what had to be done—he was going to get wet. Very wet.

Ross took a deep breath, opened the door, and stepped out into water that lapped over the top of his knees.

"Can I help you?" he shouted.

"I'm looking for Dr. Reeder—do you know if he's evacuated? I was told he might still be here." The man on the porch had on long swim trunks, high boots and a long-sleeved blue shirt with the Port Provident Beach Patrol logo on it. The shirt stuck to him so closely and was so wet that it reminded Ross of a seal's skin.

"I'm Dr. Reeder. Hold on—let me come up to the porch."

Ross turned around and saw water lapping on the driver's side floorboard where he'd opened the door. More surprising than that was the look on Becca's face. Fear had flooded into her wide eyes just like the water pooling in the truck.

"I'm going to go see what he needs. Are you okay to sit here for just a second? Then I'll get you upstairs to the garage apartment. It'll be dry up there, I promise. It's twelve feet off the ground."

Her gaze locked on the water streaming in the car, but she nodded affirmatively. Ross thought he heard an "*mmm-hmm*" through her tightly-pursed lips, but he wasn't one hundred percent sure.

"Okay. I'll be back as soon as I can for you and Cookie and Polly. Just hold on."

She nodded again, and Ross fought against the door, trying to close it. With a little more effort, it latched. Ross walked away from the frightened woman and dogs, trying to shake the uneasy feeling that had taken up residence in his heart.

The man on the porch stuck out his hand for the quickest of greetings. "I'm Rigo Vasquez, Chief of the Port Provident Beach Patrol. My team and I have been out doing water rescues, and I don't have to tell you that things are getting bad—you can see it for yourself. I just moved several people from the Sand Ridge apartments to the shelter at the high school, but there are two cats that had to be left behind. They're not allowed at the shelter."

Ross nodded. "I know. I've got an extra Labrador in my truck because of it."

"Councilwoman Angela Ruiz said she saw Becca Collins from the animal shelter in line for the last evacuation bus an hour or so ago. So, I know the shelter's not an option. Chris Lansdowne on my team said you might still be here and could possibly help us with these animals. My first responsibility is obviously to the people of Port Provident, but I just can't leave these cats to die if there's something I can do about it."

"Die? You really think it's going to be that bad, Chief?" In spite of the soaking rain all around, Ross couldn't keep his mind from snapping back—lightning fast—to the scorching sands of Iraq. His time of dancing with death was supposed to be over.

Ross guessed he'd assumed wrong.

"The storm surge is rising faster and higher than anyone thought.

It's going to be a long and dangerous night." Rigo spoke flatly. There wasn't any embellishment needed.

"So how can I help?" He was stuck on this island and in his garage apartment because he wasn't leaving Cookie or Polly—or Becca—behind. The only option was to do what he could for the rest of those in the same situation.

"Can you take these cats? With the shelter closed, we don't have any other options."

"We'll take the cats. Becca Collins is with me." Ross pointed back at his truck.

It felt strange to say that, but it looked like they were a team now. They may have had their differences, but there was no doubt that Ross and Becca both cared a great deal for the animals in this community.

Maybe that would be enough to get them through the next several hours without being at each other's throats.

"Can you come with me to get them?" Rigo asked. The apartments aren't far. We can take my truck, that way we'll have the boat if we can't get all the way there."

"Give me a minute to get Becca and Cookie, and Polly settled in the garage apartment and then we can go. Meet me in the back alley. My garage is painted light blue, like the house."

He and Chief Vasquez worked out a few minor details and then they each waded back to their respective trucks.

Back at the truck, Ross pulled forcefully on the door and then awkwardly climbed back inside. He needed even more force to shut the door behind him.

"What's going on?" Becca's voice still sounded unsure but was at least no longer so quiet that he could barely hear her.

"That's Chief Rigo Vasquez with the Beach Patrol. They had to evacuate the Sand Ridge apartments, and there are some pets left behind that he needs us to take in."

Ross carefully put the truck back in drive and pulled away from the curb, around Rigo's truck. He soon took two short right turns and drove back along the alley to his garage.

"Where are they?"

"Still at the apartments. I'm going to get you and the dogs settled and then go with him to get them."

He clicked the button on the opener to the garage and watched the garage door slide upward. As it did so, he noticed the items stored on low shelves in his garage were already floating in the water, freed from the organization that had existed just hours before. Ross pulled straight in and silently prayed that he wouldn't hit anything that would cause more trouble than they were already in for. At least inside the garage, there wasn't water pouring down.

Ross got out of the truck and then signaled for Cookie to hop on the front seat. He reached out and scooped up a hundred pounds of cream-colored Lab, then sloshed toward the stairs to the garage apartment. Cookie scampered up the stairs and bolted through the dog entrance in the front door.

One down, two to go.

When he got back to the garage, Ross saw Becca trying to open the passenger side door.

"Becca, stay put." Ross raised his voice to be heard over the noise of the storm. "Let me get Polly upstairs with Cookie, and then I'll come get you."

Becca took her hands off the door, then patted the driver's side seat, trying to coax Polly to take the same exit as Cookie had. The dog could have been Cookie's twin. She hesitated at first, then Ross whistled, and Polly's ears perked up. She placed two paws in the seat, then took a hesitant step and came to sit on the driver's seat.

Ross reached in and slid his arm under Polly's hips and shoulders. She was slightly lighter than Cookie, but she was a wet mess and slipped a little as she wiggled in his arms. Polly walked a little more slowly up the stairs, then hesitated at the dog door.

"It's ok, girl. Go on through. Cookie's in there." At Ross' gentle insistence, Polly sniffed the door and pushed her muzzle on the weighted plastic flap. Quickly, she forced herself the rest of the way through.

Ross turned and headed back to the truck. One more passenger to see to safety.

He waded over to Becca's door. She waved him off.

"I'm coming with you."

Never in a million years had he planned on weathering a hurricane with Becca Collins. But now that she was here, in his truck, feet from his apartment…well, Ross felt a deep responsibility to keep her safe.

"Becca, you need to stay here. You can see it for yourself. It's not safe out there."

"If it's not safe for me, then it's not safe for you, either."

"I'll be fine. I'll be with Chief Vasquez."

She raised her eyebrows. "See? I'll be fine too. Since I'll also be with Chief Vasquez."

Ross pushed his fingers through his hair. This is how every conversation with Becca went. Things started out fine, then she got unreasonable. So much for that short-lived protective streak he felt for her.

Everything was back to normal. Except for the weather.

"I don't have time to argue with you, Becca. Chief Vasquez is waiting, and this storm is not."

She pushed the passenger door open and poised herself to get out. "So, it's settled, then?"

They could see the apartments, but they couldn't reach them by truck. The water was just too deep through here.

"If I go ahead," Chief Vasquez said, "I'm going to stall out my truck and never get it started again. So, we'll need to take the boat."

"I'll help," Ross quickly volunteered, and both of the men got out of the Beach Patrol truck.

Becca climbed over the console and hopped in the front seat, ready to join them. Ross hadn't said much to her on the way over, although he'd asked several questions of Chief Vasquez. That was fine. She didn't need the grumpy vet's approval anyway.

She'd stopped trying to figure out Ross Reeder a long time ago.

As she scooted out of the truck, the water felt like the contents of a bathtub that had sat too long. It was vaguely temperate, but trending toward cool. The color was deeply brown, like yesterday's coffee grounds, and Becca surrendered all hope for the white tennis shoes she was wearing. She knew that much like Port Provident, her shoes would never be the same again.

She held to the side of the truck bed as she carefully walked back toward the two men.

"Becca, if you can climb up on the rear bumper here, we'll hold the boat steady while you get in."

Rigo closed the tailgate with one hand as he spoke, then maneuvered the small jon boat parallel with the bumper of the truck. Becca gripped one hand around the edge of the bed of the truck and boosted herself up.

She flopped into the boat rather ungracefully but reminded herself that she didn't need Ross Reeder's approval—and that extended to her gracefulness in a boat. She'd already slipped and fallen once today anyway. He probably thought she was a grade-A klutz. And she was okay with that. He didn't need to know the personal details of her life.

Because she didn't care what he thought of her.

"Becca? Are you okay?" Ross boosted himself into the boat next.

"Fine. These shoes are a little slippery, that's all." She'd blame it on the shoes. That was perfectly believable.

Rigo got in, pushed the boat back from the truck, and started the engine. The rain fought them at every foot they tried to advance, but they eventually made it back to the apartment complex. Rigo angled up next to a rusted metal staircase and tied a sturdy knot to moor the small boat.

"I left them up here in 408."

He got out first, followed by Ross. When it was Becca's turn to get out, Rigo held the side of the boat, trying to keep it steady.

Ross held out his hand. "Let me help you, Becca."

She tried to wave off his offer. "I'm okay."

"No one pays attention when I stretch out my hand," he muttered.

"What? You make no sense."

"It's from the Bible. Proverbs 1:24. There really isn't time for a Sunday school lesson. Can you just give me your hand, Becca?"

What kind of person quoted the Bible in the middle of a hurricane? Bess would have, Becca reminded herself. But Bess was special. She wasn't anything like Ross Reeder. "I told you, I'm okay."

"These stairs are just as slippery as the bumper." Without waiting for her to say anything in reply, he leaned back into the boat, put his hands around Becca's waist, and pulled her out.

She'd noticed his hands earlier, but as they circled her waist, she did a lot more than notice them. Her shirt was soaked through with the deluge of Hope, but the warmth of his palms soaked through the wet cloth and warmed her skin.

Ross pivoted and swung her behind him, placing her carefully two steps up where the stairs were not under water.

"Um, thank you," Becca said, still acutely aware of the elevated temperature where his palms had pressed above her hip bones.

"You're welcome."

"Okay, team. Let's go." Rigo scooted around both Becca and Ross and led the way to apartment 408. The door was marked with a blue X, drawn on with spray paint.

Becca stared at the graffiti. "Have people already started looting? What is that?"

Rigo gave a hard shove to the door and forced it open. "It means this home has been checked. We're trying to go door-to-door and make sure everyone is getting to the shelter, if possible."

Becca saw a carpeted climbing tower, but there was no sign of any cats. "I guess they're hiding."

"Probably. They were pretty shook up when I left. The door's been shut, though, so I know they're still in here," Rigo said.

"Becca, you take the living room and dining area. I'll take the bedroom and closet. Rigo, can you check the other areas?" Ross took charge of the situation.

"Sure. I'll look in the bathroom and the hall closet first." Rigo walked down the hallway, and Ross followed him.

Becca stood in the middle of the room for a moment, listening for a sound, a clue. In a short moment, she heard a faint mewling. Lowering herself to all fours, Becca scooted toward the couch and lifted the red-and-blue plaid ruffle around the bottom, then looked underneath. It was dark under there, but she could easily make out two green eyes.

She reached out her hands, but the kitten was just out of arm's reach and wouldn't budge on its own.

"Found one, but I can't get to it. Can one of you help me move the couch?"

Ross answered. "Coming. I found the other one behind the shoes in the back of the closet."

He turned the corner and came back into the living room, one orange-and-white kitten tucked securely between his elbow and his shirt. The furball wiggled a bit, and Ross stroked the kitten's head gently and reassuringly.

Laying the cat in the corner of an upholstered chair, Ross picked up the end of the couch closest to Becca. She wiggled closer to the kitten, then touched the soft fur. With a gentle tug, she scooped the cat into her hands and pulled it from the hiding place.

"Got 'em both," Rigo said. "Let's go."

Ross scooped his kitten out of the chair and stopped for a second in front of Becca and her kitten. A gust of wind howled like a banshee outside and rattled the window. The kitten tried to burrow more deeply into Ross' arms. Ross reached out and rubbed his pointer finger from side-to-side between the kitten's ears.

Becca's mind flashed back to how securely Ross had held her a few minutes before as he pulled her out of the boat.

She wasn't jealous of a kitten—that would be crazy.

But as the winds continued their thrashing, she reluctantly admitted that a little reassurance was a good thing right now.

Even if that reassurance came from a man, she'd long ago deemed "least likely to daydream about."

~

"Rigo! Stop!" The voice in the back seat was edgy with panic.

"That's easier said than done, Becca. Why?" Rigo stayed calm. Ross wasn't surprised. The man headed up Beach Patrol—the law enforcement division responsible for all the lifeguarding, water rescues and more in Port Provident. He'd probably seen it all.

"There's another cat on the porch rail of that red house ahead to the left. We can't just leave it out in this storm!"

The two kittens in Becca's lap meowed softly in agreement.

"Ross, you want me to try and stop?" Rigo glanced at the passenger seat, then immediately turned his stare back to the flooded road.

"Ross—we can't just drive by. We have to stop. We have to. That cat will die." Becca pushed more stress, more emotion into every sentence.

The rain continued to come down in sheets. They were four houses from the clinic, and Ross strongly wanted to get back to Cookie. The furry veteran of war had a hard time with spring showers. This would be his companion's biggest test since Iraq, and Ross did not want to leave Cookie alone any longer than necessary.

"Please, Ross."

Becca's voice had sounded so strong only seconds before, but now Ross heard a quiver in the plea.

Ross took a deep breath. Cookie would be okay for another few minutes.

"Let us out wherever you can, Rigo, and we'll go get the cat. We'll get back to the house ourselves." Ross unbuckled his seatbelt. "Hand me the kittens, Becca. I think I can put them inside my shirt. We're probably going to need all hands free to make this work."

Rigo slowed down and pulled as close to the high curb as possible. It was a difficult task. As he maneuvered the truck, Becca handed the two rescued kittens to Ross, one at a time.

Ross felt the brush of kitten fur as Becca handed them off. He was used to cats—he petted cat fur countless times a day. But the whisper-light touch of Becca's palm as it crossed his felt entirely unexpected-- soft and chilled from the rain and storm.

She passed off the second kitten, but this time, there was no connection between their hands. As he tucked the second cat inside his

T-shirt, Ross couldn't place why he felt like something was missing—but he did.

"Ready, Becca?" Ross placed his hand on the handle to open the door.

Becca did the same in the back seat. "Ready. Let's go get a cat."

"Rigo, thanks, man. We'll take good care of these kittens. Stay safe out there."

"Thanks, Ross—I will. Y'all don't need to stay out. Get the cat, then get to your place and get as high as you can. The water is going to keep rising, and it's going to be getting really dark soon. It's going to be a long, dangerous night. I mean it—no matter what else you see, get only this cat and then go to your house and stay inside. Call me if there's something else that needs to be taken care of—but at some point, even I'm not going to be able to be out doing rescues—and that means for neither man nor beast."

Ross felt it as soon as he stepped out of the truck. The water swirled around his legs—a certified river, where once there had been an ordinary street. The top of the water was coated with the rainbow sheen of spilled gasoline and clumps of floating ants and trash. He didn't want to think about what drifted lower under the surface.

He steadied one hand underneath the kittens in the bowl of his tucked-in shirt and extended the other to Becca as she tentatively found her footing outside of the truck. As soon as the doors shut, Rigo pulled away. Becca held on to Ross' hand, pulling him in the other direction—back toward the cat.

Ross jerked her back, and she slipped off the curb and splashed backward. "Watch out, Becca!"

"What?" she sputtered. "What was that for?"

He let go of Becca's hand and gestured at the S-shaped swirl a few yards past.

"Moccasin."

Becca let out a scream and flailed back toward Ross, bumping into the side of his chest. She was soaked through, but he could feel the soft curves beneath the sticky T-shirt.

"Come on, let's go," Ross said. He needed to focus on something other than curves—both the S-curve of the snake's motion and the other ones he'd become acutely aware of.

One set of curves definitely scared him far more than the other.

Becca shook her head.

"I can't." Her teeth gave a *ch-ch-chatter*, and her voice was so low he could barely hear the objection.

"Becca, it's pouring. We're in the middle of a mess. We have to go." She still hesitated.

"I have wet cats in my shirt, Becca." He held out his free hand, hoping she would take it, but she didn't. "Please come on."

She looked up at him, her eyes wide as they locked on his. "Do you think there are more?"

The answer was an unequivocal yes. But the truth wasn't going to help this situation. Instead of lying to her, he placed his hand between her shoulder blades and applied a gentle pressure.

"We've got to get this cat and get inside. Becca, look at me."

Her eyes were dark like chocolate cake, but in the downpour of Hurricane Hope and the gray of the skies above, they looked almost black. Now they looked utterly stripped of the bravado she'd displayed when she'd begged Rigo to stop the truck for one more rescue. Even though snakes weren't high on his list either, Ross knew Becca spent all day around all types of animals. He didn't expect this kind of reaction from her.

She kept her gaze focused upon his face, but Ross could tell she was looking through him. "When I was little, my mother's boyfriend had a snake. He would lock me in the closet and put the snake's cage right outside the door so that I didn't try and escape." The narrowest ribbon of liquid lined her lower eyelid. Her voice dropped even lower. "I hate snakes."

Ross couldn't believe what she'd just revealed. He couldn't believe the far-away fear he heard in her voice. And he couldn't believe that anything Becca Collins could tell him would scare him more than standing in the middle of a street with water up to his knees as a hurricane blew in.

But her quiet revelation blew him away.

He adjusted the position of the kittens in his shirt, pushed them higher, so they rested more closely to his chest than his abdomen. They wriggled around at the adjustment, and he felt the downward swipe of tiny claws scratching through the uppermost layer of skin.

Ross leaned slightly, still holding the kittens at bay with his forearm, and reached his hand awkwardly behind the very top of Becca's thighs—the only part of her legs still exposed above the line of the water. He adjusted the hand that had been between her shoulder blades, taking it all the way around the front of her shoulders, squeezing the round curve at the juncture of her arm with his elbow. And then he tugged upward, picking her up and pulling her tight against his waist.

He readjusted his left arm to support under her knees, positioning her leg to pin in the cats in his shirt. Ross then waded to the porch, carrying her above whatever might have been in the water below.

Ross focused on each step, acutely aware that if he lost his footing, they both would fall. Alarm bells rang in his ears that this situation was precarious at best—in every way possible.

They sidled up to the black ball of fur sitting atop the gingerbread railing.

"Lean forward and grab the cat, then put him in your lap. I'll carry you back to the house."

As they sloshed back down the steps and back toward the house, Ross realized that he would have carried her anywhere to not hear her whispered voice filled with long-held fear ever again.

That thought scared him almost as much as the thought of whatever lurked under the water. Ross had never thought of Becca Collins as anything other than an impulsive woman with big ideas and no common sense about how to practically execute them. He'd certainly never thought of her as a scared child, locked in a closet, crouched with fear.

And he'd never thought of her as a woman with melting brown eyes that he wanted to protect from snakes and storms.

Until now.

Eventually, they reached the edge of the stairs to Ross' garage apartment. Ross gently lowered Becca to the first dry step, then peeled the kittens out of his shirt and lowered them into her waiting arms. He laughed.

"What's so funny?" Becca frowned as the water from the clouds above pelted them all with more stinging rain, each drop sharp as one of the tiny kittens' claws.

"You." Ross was still lost in his thoughts, wondering how his opinion of Becca had softened in just a matter of an hour or so. He still thought she didn't have much common sense and was full of crazy ideas—but now he saw another side to her, and he couldn't get it out of his head.

"Me?" The frown tucked in a little tighter around the corkscrewed corner of her mouth.

"You've got a bouquet of wet kittens."

She looked down at the rolling, wet mess of fur in her arms. The frown on her face melted like butter in a Texas summer, and he saw her thoughts shift far away again. Ross braced himself for another unimaginable childhood revelation.

"No one's ever brought me a bouquet before—not flowers or anything." She smiled, and this time, the look in her eyes was fully engaged in the here-and-now. "So, I guess this is where I say 'thank you, they're beautiful'—except it's just too wet for small talk."

Her smile broadened, and the roundness in her cheeks transformed her whole face, then she turned and walked up the stairs to the door. Ross stayed at the foot of the stairs, unmoving, watching Becca's ponytail streaming behind her, limp and drenched with the liquid calling card of Hurricane Hope.

She may have been joking about the beauty of the impromptu kitten bouquet—but the little furballs weren't the only thing Ross would call beautiful in the midst of this storm.

He couldn't push the thought from his mind. And as Becca tucked each cat through the little dog door that Cookie usually used, he wondered if he was about to be way in over his head—in a way that would have nothing to do with Hurricane Hope's storm surge.

*B*ecca stood in the small bathroom at the back of Ross' garage apartment. Water streamed off her hair and from the seams of her cotton shirt, then all flowed together down to the small white octagonal tile on the floor. The tiles reminded her of childhood in her grandmother's house.

Here in Port Provident, the tiles seemed vintage, a nod to all the historic homes across the island.

Back in the government-subsidized housing of Milwaukee, Wisconsin, the exact same small ceramics seemed just plain old. There, it was a constant reminder that you lived in a home that wasn't your own and there would never be any money to update or modernize.

Becca watched the puddle grow, and she herself puddled into the moment and the memories.

"You okay in there, Becca? Do you need any more towels?" Ross knocked at the wooden door.

She looked at the towel Ross had given her five minutes ago. It was still clutched in her fist.

"I don't think so. What I really want to take is a shower and rinse all this funk off of me. Do you think that's okay?"

What she really wanted to do was rinse the memories out of her mind and give herself a few more minutes alone before being unavoidably trapped in a small space with Ross Reeder as a hurricane blew through town—but "funk" would probably be a good enough explanation.

"I think if you make it fast, you certainly could. Now that you mention it, I'd like to do the same once you're through. Then I guess we should clean out the tub and fill it with water, you know, just in case."

Becca climbed in the tub, then twisted a few knobs and water began to come out of the ancient shower head above her. The problem was, it had all the pressure of a two-year-old spitting out a snack cracker. This was not going to be a very thorough shower.

But, if a few minutes in a stream of water could at least cleanse her thoughts about riding out this storm with Ross Reeder, then she'd consider the shower a success even if the funk of wading in the water in Port Provident's streets still clung to her.

After a quick scrub with the blue bar of soap next to the tub and splash after splash to try and rinse off as much as she could, Becca realized washing her hair stood no chance. Instead, she wiggled under the trickle of water and just tried to let as much of the day wash from between the strands as possible.

The rain pounded on the roof above her and Becca realized she needed to give herself a stern talking-to. Yes, she was stuck with someone who generally made her very uncomfortable. But she had a dry roof over her head, and a dry floor under her feet—her own apartment behind the animal shelter would most assuredly be underwater soon, if it wasn't flooded already.

Plus, that same frustrating man had carried cats in his shirt for her. He'd helped her save defenseless animals in the face of treacherous conditions and given them all—herself and Polly the dog included—shelter from the storm without asking any questions.

In spite of their many tangles and arguments, Ross Reeder loved animals just like she did. And that had to be worth something. If she could just focus on that—what they had in common—maybe she could get through the next few hours.

Ross continued organizing the small stockpile in his kitchen. He hadn't planned on staying in Port Provident during the storm, and as he looked around him, he realized that he was not very well prepared for riding out a hurricane. He knew it wouldn't be long until they faced the inevitable interruptions to power and water and anything else that made living in a city preferable to living in an Army camp in Iraq.

Before the night was over, Ross was pretty sure that he'd be well-reminded of his time on the other side of the world without creature comforts.

Then he corrected himself. He might be without comforts, but there were plenty of creatures to go around. The small garage apartment was stuffed with two Labrador retrievers and three cats.

And one Becca Collins.

As if she knew she'd crossed his thoughts, she crossed into the room. She wore a pair of black and red athletic shorts and an oversized gray T-shirt with a faded logo in the middle. Her long hair was pulled back in a high ponytail and was still soaking wet.

"I think I've got a hairdryer in a cabinet somewhere," Ross said.

"It's ok. It'll dry sooner or later," she said, touching the ends of her hair self-consciously.

"While you were in the shower, I waded through the garage as best I could and brought up whatever I could find that I thought we might need. And I got the extra dog food for Polly that had been left down there." Ross gestured toward the soggy pile sitting on towels in the living room. "I wish I'd thought to bring up my car insurance paperwork because I'm pretty sure I'll be making a claim on that tomorrow."

"You think it's done?"

"I don't see how it survives. The water is to the tops of the tires already, and we haven't even seen the worst of what Hurricane Hope is bringing."

Becca sat heavily in the green recliner in the living room. Polly ambled toward her and laid her muzzle gently on Becca's knee.

"What next?" She patted the dog's head absently. "Do we just wait?"

Ross remembered a young private on his staff in Iraq asking the same question during one long, dark night. They'd known something was coming. They just didn't know what or when. It wound up being the night he met Cookie, the night Cookie's handler had been blown up by an IED that threatened to take the heroic dog's life as well.

Ross sucked in a slow breath, remembering the hot desert air and the impending sense that you couldn't control what was to come.

"Yeah. I think we do what we can to prepare. Then we wait. It'll all be over by morning."

Becca turned her head slightly to face him. "So, what should we do to prepare?"

"I guess I'm going to go take the quickest shower ever before we lose water. Then I'll clean and fill the tub. I've got some boxed mac and cheese in the kitchen. Do you think you could make up a big bowl so we'll have something to eat later? I've got a lot of bachelor food like sodas and chips, too. We'll at least be able to eat something tonight and tomorrow, and then we'll go from there."

Mentally, he added the disclaimer that he'd have been better prepared if he'd had any intention of staying, but Ross decided voicing that statement wouldn't help anyone right now. Becca looked more frightened than Cookie, who had curled up in a ball in the far back corner of his dog crate.

"Okay, I can do that. Anything else?"

"Try loading as much of the food from the fridge and freezer into those coolers I brought up. They're the rugged outdoor style that will keep things cold for close to 100 hours. Just pack them tightly and spread the ice from the ice maker on top."

"Got it. Now go get your shower and get that tub filled. I don't feel like we have much time."

Ross had boarded up the windows of the apartment yesterday so nothing would get broken and ruined in his absence. But he ran out of plywood before he could cover the small two-by-two window over the sink in the kitchen. There had been no more plywood to buy on the island to cover up the tiny square, so Ross had just decided to hope for the best.

Now, he was strangely glad to have a view to the outside world. It helped him feel like he knew what he was up against. The tone of the sky had begun to shift to green behind the gray swathes of clouds.

It was ominous, to be sure. Ross thought that if he'd had a long ponytail of his own, he'd probably be absently toying with it, just like Becca continued to do. Anything to ease the anxiety he felt building up as the barometric pressure across Provident Island continued to fall.

"I'll be out in less than five minutes, Becca. Don't worry."

She walked into the galley-style kitchen and was silhouetted in the eerie light coming from the small, uncovered window.

"I'm not worried," she said. Then her voice lowered, and she chewed her bottom lip between her teeth. "Terrified is a better word."

Deep in his heart, Ross completely understood. But even though he'd been discharged from the Army, once an officer, always an officer.

And an officer never let down those he commanded.

Even when his command was two Labradors, three cats, and one woman with hauntingly expressive eyes and a very wet ponytail.

Becca couldn't tear her gaze away from the rolling boil of water in the pot on the stove. She needed to pour in the pasta and quit wasting time, but she couldn't help but wonder if this was what the surf looked like, only a few blocks away.

She remembered standing on a stool in her grandmother's kitchen as a child, stirring half-curved noodles in a pot much like this one. She'd learned to cook for herself at an early age—too early, in fact.

She'd learned to dodge danger at an early age as well. But nothing like this, she thought as she looked at the changing color of the sky and band after band after band of clouds in a line that rolled in from the Gulf.

Nothing ever like this.

"I've got the tub cleaned out and filling up. At least we'll have some extra water for us and all these animals." Ross' voice startled Becca out of her thoughts about the clouds of her past and the very different clouds of her present. "It's a bit like the ark in here, isn't it?"

She gave a short laugh. "I guess so. I remember my grandmother reading me a book about that when I was a kid. I remember all the pictures of the animals. I don't remember if they made it to dry land or not, though."

"They did," Ross said matter-of-factly. "I was fascinated with the story of the ark as a kid. Boats, animals. There was a lot there to hold my imagination. Even then, I knew I wanted to help animals. I just never dreamed that I'd be marching them two-by-two into my own house and saving them from the rising waters."

Becca took the pot of pasta off the stove and dumped it into a colander in the sink to drain. "I should just call you Noah, huh? That was his name, right?"

"Yeah, it was. Call me Noah."

She transferred the noodles to a large bowl and began to stir in powdered cheese and milk to make the sauce. "Eh, I'm used to calling you Dr. No. So, Noah won't be too much of a stretch. No-uh."

The wind gave a howl outside as a gust whipped down the street. Ross could see a giant palm tree branch go flying through the air.

"Dr. No?"

She shrugged and continued to stir. "Yeah. It's your favorite word in board meetings, and you are a doctor."

Ross felt the hair along the back of his neck bristle at her implication. "Hey, I take my responsibilities on that board seriously, Becca."

"No doubt you do, Ross. Emphasis on the 'no'."

"Just because I don't rubber stamp every hair-brained scheme you have—like Tanya Parkington does—that doesn't make me some kind of roadblock. I have a fiduciary duty to the animal shelter. We can't spend what we can't afford."

Becca scraped the bowl with the edge of the spoon. The rasping noise of stainless steel on stainless steel screeched throughout the small house.

"We can't fulfill our mission in this community in a run-down shack of a building that barely meets code and was past capacity two years ago," she said through gritted teeth.

"And you can't make me out to be the bad guy at every single board meeting just because you don't like my viewpoint on things."

Becca looked at Ross point-blank. He'd seen that look of steely, focused determination on snipers in the Army.

And then, he saw nothing at all.

A loud pop! sounded outside and the whole house went black, save the greenish glow haunting the small kitchen window.

"There goes the electricity. Well, here we go into the long, dark night of Hurricane Hope."

Becca made a muffled noise under her breath. Ross thought it was agreement, but he couldn't say for sure.

"Stay put, and I'll go light the candles."

"Okay. I'll just finish what I can in here."

Ross heard some scuffling and turning sounds, then Becca spoke again. "Looks like the water is out now, too. There's nothing coming out of the sink. I'd apologize in advance for leaving your stockpot without rinsing it out, but come tomorrow morning, I think a pot with stuck-on pasta is probably going to be the least of your worries."

Ross moved around the corners of the room, setting out candles that he'd brought up from the garage, then lighting them. As he came to the back of the room, he could hear Cookie breathing heavily in his crate.

A low, rumbling howl filled the room, like the sound of a locomotive gathering steam as it moved closer and faster.

"What is that?" Becca asked.

Ross knelt in front of the wire door to the crate. "It's Cookie."

"Is everything okay?"

Ross held a candle low and tried to illuminate the crate without being invasive. "No. Cookie has Canine PTSD."

Ross became aware of the sound of Becca's footsteps shuffling across the room. "Canine PTSD? I've never even heard of such a thing."

"It's not formally recognized in veterinary circles at this point." Ross kept his voice low and steady. "But I know it's real. I've seen it first-hand. Our military dogs in the field, like Cookie, experience the same stresses and dangers that our soldiers do. It's only natural that they experience the same reactions."

Becca squatted down near Ross. Polly sauntered over as well, sniffing the air. She sat cautiously behind Becca.

"Cookie was your dog in Iraq?"

"No, not my dog. Cookie was the working partner of Sergeant Bart Thompson. Sergeant Thompson stepped on an IED while he and Cookie were patrolling ahead of a unit. He was killed instantly. Cookie was brought to me, and I did what I could for him."

The low growl continued. It didn't take overhead illumination to see the fear in Cookie's black, round eyes. Candlelight was enough.

"Becca, there's a tennis ball in the plastic crate at the end of the couch." Ross pointed behind him. "Could you bring it over here?"

"Sure." Becca crab-crawled backward a few paces and retrieved the ball, then placed it in Ross' outstretched hand.

Slowly, Ross reached his hand inside the crate, palm outstretched fully and facing up, with the tennis ball perched right in the center. "Sssh, Cookie. It's okay. Here's your binky-ball."

"What's the tennis ball for?" Becca kept her voice barely above a whisper. Ross appreciated that she stayed calm. Although she'd said she didn't know about Canine PTSD, she'd probably seen plenty of scared dogs at the shelter. It made him breathe a little easier, knowing Becca wouldn't do anything to upset the delicate balance right now.

"You know how a pacifier calms babies down?"

"Mmm-hmm."

"This ball is like Cookie's pacifier. If he can just hold it in his teeth, it tends to reassure him."

The dog sniffed at the green fuzzy ball in Ross' hand, then took it gently into his mouth. The growling stopped. Instantly, relief washed over Ross with an intensity which mirrored the waves topping the seawall on Gulfview Boulevard.

Since the moment he met Cookie, they'd shared a bond. He'd

promised Cookie on an operating table in Iraq that he wouldn't let the dog down. It had taken almost two years, wading through a lot of red tape, and more than a few sleepless nights before he'd fulfilled that promise to Cookie as thoroughly as he could. And although he was no longer officially in the Army, Ross took his vow to Cookie as seriously as the one he'd once made to defend America and the Constitution.

Cookie was as much a brother on the battlefield as all the two-legged creatures Ross had deployed alongside.

Ross stood up and backed away. Becca followed his lead. Almost as soon as the low rumble from Cookie came to an end, though, one from outside began as the winds picked up and beat against the sides of the garage apartment.

Cookie began to shift position in the crate. Ross could hear the sound of fur brushing against the plastic wall. At the sound, Polly stood up and walked to the front of the crate and gave it a sniff, then blew out a staccato breath through her nostrils. Cookie answered back with a sniff of his own.

Polly pushed at the wire door with her nose and laid down, feet and head inside the crate.

"She's got his six," Ross said with amazement.

"What?" Becca asked.

Ross turned to face her, adjusting the candle nearby so he could see her better. "It's a military term. It means 'got your back.' It's a saying that developed during World War I, where a pilot would take up the six o'clock position behind another pilot, as a means of covering behind him. Now it's come to symbolize loyalty and cooperation and support."

He saw her face soften in the candlelight. She smiled and looked fondly at the gentle tail wag of the light-colored Labrador. "Yeah, I'd say you're right. Polly's most certainly got Cookie's six."

The small apartment swayed a bit as the wind continued to pound.

It hit Ross that it would be a long night. He hadn't ever been through a hurricane before. He didn't really know what was ahead. He thought back to their conversation in the kitchen a few minutes earlier. They undeniably had a past. And normally, he would not consider Becca Collins a friend. "Co-worker" was stretching it. Even "acquaintance" felt like too endearing of a term for most of their encounters in their respective roles at the Port Provident Animal Shelter.

But tonight, he knew they'd have to set all that aside.

"Becca?"

She looked away from the dogs in the corner. "Yes?"

"Look…I don't exactly know what's to come tonight. I'm an Army brat. I grew up on military bases all over the world. Germany isn't exactly hurricane-prone, and neither is RAF Lakenheath in England."

She gave a throaty chuckle. It sounded strong, like her usual personality, but smooth. "Neither is Wisconsin."

"So, we're on the same page?"

Becca tilted her head slightly, making her ponytail sway. "I think so?"

"What I mean is, I don't know what's going to happen tonight. If this storm is as big as Rick O'Connell and National Weather News say it's going to be, we could have to make some big decisions, some quick decisions. We're going to have to work together and not be hung up in the arguments of the past." He reached out his hand, much like he'd done for Cookie only minutes before. "Becca, I've got your six tonight, if you've got mine."

He couldn't explain why, but it felt like his breath couldn't squeeze past his Adam's apple. It was stuck there, just waiting for Becca's answer.

She put out her own hand and wrapped her fingers around Ross', then shook gently. Air filled back into his lungs and all the thoughts in his mind filled with the shapes of the flickering candlelight as they reflected in the glassy curve of her eyes.

"What rank were you? In the Army, I mean?"

He hadn't expected to care so genuinely about what her answer would be. And he hadn't expected her to ask a question about his past.

"Major. Why?"

She nodded, and the shy smile came back across her lips. The same candlelight that refracted in her eyes filled the curve of a dimple in her left cheek, causing the play of light and shadow on her face.

"I've got your six, Major Reeder."

Ross couldn't tear his eyes away from the small square of sky visible from the kitchen. It surprised him that there wasn't much thunder or lightning that accompanied the eerie glow behind the rows of clouds that stretched from one end of the island to the other, rolling relentlessly northward.

"I don't know what I expected. I don't think it was this," he said out loud—as much to himself as to Becca.

She shone a flashlight into an overhead kitchen cabinet she'd opened. "What'd you expect?"

"I lived in San Antonio for a while. One spring, the craziest storm blew through. It was everything legend says spring squalls in Texas are. It came out of nowhere, dumped rain, boomed thunder. Streaks of lightning broke the sky and made you jump as the sound cracked around you. There were even a few tornadoes not far from the base. It was loud and bossy—kind of like you."

Ross leaned back slightly and made sure Becca could see the smile on his face as he said the last line.

She threw back a glance full of side-eye. "You're expecting me to disagree with that assessment, aren't you?"

"Well, I've never seen a woman take 'bossy' as a compliment."

She reached in the cabinet and pulled out two bowls from the back corner. They were sitting on the top shelf, but Becca reached them with ease.

"If I wasn't bossy, I'd have wound up as a prostitute hanging around a crack house. I'm thankful I've got a mind of my own and the ability to say no."

She dished the mac and cheese out of the mixing bowl and divided it into individual portions. Ross thought she might have filled the bowls with extra emphasis, but he couldn't say for sure.

He also couldn't say for sure if she was serious. Prostitution? Crack houses? Surely she was speaking in hyperbole.

Then again, he'd seen plenty of things in Iraq—and been told first-hand accounts of many more—things you'd have to see to believe, but once you'd seen them, the memories never left you.

Memories like that affected anyone—or anything—with a mind. Like Cookie, curled in the corner of his crate, chewing on a tennis ball to help soothe the anxiety he had because the deafening sound of the wind and the rain reminded him of the night he'd lost his handler on the side of a road half a world away.

"You said earlier you're from Wisconsin?" Maybe he could figure out a way to ask without really asking.

"Milwaukee. The projects, specifically, if that's what you're getting at. I wasn't throwing out the observation for shock value. That's who my mother was. But that's not who I am." Becca's voice carried clearly over the constant roar and drum of the storm just beyond the walls of the garage apartment.

She handed him a bowl, then scooted past him with her own, headed for the recliner in the living room.

"No, you're definitely not." Ross had thought of her as a lot of things during their acquaintance, but never had he thought of her with the sorrow and defiance that he heard clearly in her voice. "So how did you wind up in Texas from Wisconsin?"

Ross pulled a chair from the dining room table near to the recliner. His living quarters were definitely a bachelor pad—he rarely entertained, so his hodge-podge of furniture skewed strongly toward being functional for a man and his dog, and not much else.

"A bus," she replied, matter-of-factly. "I looked at a map of all the places that buses were leaving the station for. Port Provident was the farthest away from Milwaukee. I didn't know anything about Texas or Port Provident, but the fact that it was twelve-hundred miles and almost twenty hours away sounded perfect to me."

Ross finished a bite of mac and cheese before continuing the conversation. "So, you just wanted to get away?"

"Yeah. You would have too."

He nodded. "I felt that way about Iraq."

Becca poked at her pasta with a fork but didn't actually eat. "You could draw a number of comparisons between my childhood and a war zone."

"I'm sorry." It seemed like the only appropriate thing to say. He'd seen war first-hand. He'd also had a very secure, loving childhood. If Becca couldn't relate love and kindness to her growing-up years, then Ross truly was sorry. Every kid deserved to be a kid—free from worry and loss.

Even kids who grew up to be headstrong, argumentative adults.

"It's okay. I mean, it's not like you had anything to do with it. It just was what it was. Everyone has their own path in life. This was mine."

"So, do you like it here in Texas?" Ross wondered if she felt like her big gamble to get on a bus to a destination she'd never heard of was worth it. He'd done a few things in his day and had seen a few more, but he wasn't sure he had that kind of spirit of adventure tucked inside.

Becca looked up and turned her head to the side. The still-damp ponytail fell over her shoulder and left a mark on the gray of her T-shirt that seemed even larger than it was, thanks to the dim candlelight.

"I found myself here," she said, with a hint of emotion. "I came to the edge. I came to where the water meets the land, to where I couldn't go any farther. And at that boundary, I found who I am."

"And who is that?"

"A good person. A responsible person. A person who tries to help those who can't help themselves—the animals of Provident Island." She kept her stare focused. "In short, not my mother."

The defiance in her words hung in the air between them like one of the angry clouds pushing outside.

Ross stood up and took his bowl to the kitchen. He wouldn't be doing dishes tonight, but doing something mundane like straightening up took his mind off everything that swirled around him.

The wind made the narrow garage apartment reverberate like a plucked guitar string. As the time and darkness and howling wore on, Ross became more and more aware of how everything could change in an instant.

"Becca, can you dig in that white box at the back of the room? I think there are some batteries in there. I remembered I've got a radio at the back of the closet that will run on some double-As. I think we need to turn it on and see if we can hear anything about what's happening. I'd do just about anything for a generator and a TV with an antenna right about now, just for the chance that we might find a signal."

Becca headed toward the box in the back while Ross headed for the closet in the opposite direction. When they'd both found what they were looking for, they came back to the kitchen, still lit with the colors of the clouds and the glow of candles.

"Where is Polly's special dog food? It's way past time to feed her. I can get some food for Cookie too, if you'll tell me where that is. Oh, and do you have any cat food? Not that I've even seen any of the cats since we got back to the house, but I figure we need to put something out for them, in case they get brave enough or hungry enough to come out."

Ross pointed back at the stash of supplies Becca had just dug through. "Polly's food is hiding behind those plastic boxes. You probably just missed it. Cookie's is in the kitchen, at the bottom of the pantry. I've got a bag of cat food in there, too, because there are always cats hanging around here."

Becca filled bowls as Ross fiddled with the radio. The scene struck him as almost domestic, like something straight out of an episode of 1950s television.

Well, it might have been, if he hadn't been Ross Reeder and she hadn't been Becca Collins, and they hadn't both been surrounded by a hurricane. That combination together would never mix into any kind of domestic bliss, even if he had come to learn new information about Becca tonight that had given him pause for thought.

The radio crackled to life as Ross adjusted the batteries and twisted the dial.

"It's staticky, but I hear something, Becca." Some of the tension that had built up in his veins flowed back out at the sound of a connection—however small—to the outside world.

"Be right there. Let me just fill these bowls for all the animals."

As Ross played with the dial, trying to find the station with the best sound quality, Becca took bowls of food to Polly and Cookie.

As Becca crossed back to the kitchen area where Ross stood, a familiar voice came through the small speaker clearly. It was a press conference with Port Provident's Mayor Blankenship.

"Because all rescues were suspended more than an hour ago, and conditions on all of Provident Island are deteriorating more rapidly than we had predicted, we are asking all of our citizens who have remained behind to label their arms with their Social Security Number, for possible identification purposes. Please use a permanent marker that won't wash off."

The uncovered window in the kitchen rattled violently with a gust, punctuating the seriousness of the message they'd just heard. All the anxiety Ross had managed to get settled came flooding back with the same force of the swirling water in the streets below.

Becca looked at him. Her eyes were wider and darker than even Cookie's.

"Oh my gosh," she whispered. Her breath made the flame on the nearby candle flutter. "What are we going to do, Ross? Mayor Blankenship just basically said we're going to die tonight."

4

---

*E*ven though Ross had tried explaining the practicality of the mayor's statement, Becca couldn't stop shivering.

Ross came around behind her and wrapped his arms around her, gently squeezing the tops of her arms and the area just under her collarbone with his strong forearms. As stunned as she was by the announcement that had crackled through the radio, it stunned Becca even more to realize that the chill in her bones had warmed at the simple touch from Ross.

It stunned her even more than that when she leaned her head softly back against his chest. The curve at the base of her skull fit in the divot between his pectoral muscles. She felt the pull, like a magnet, holding her next to him. She didn't want to move.

She didn't want to think about Ross Reeder's strong arms or supportive chest or the way that he calmed her down without saying a word. Those thoughts would have normally scared her—Ross Reeder was not the kind of guy she had any interest in—but right now, everything else around her scared her more.

If the mayor's prediction was correct—and Becca couldn't think of a reason why Mayor Blankenship would be lying—then none of it mattered. Not the fights they'd had, not the different viewpoints they'd held, not any of the things that had been important twenty-four hours ago.

"Becca," Ross said calmly. "It's going to be okay."

She shook her head like a wet dog. "No. No, it's not. You heard her."

"Becca. This is not the end for us."

Even at a time like this, he was throwing out the contrarian statements. No matter how his arms felt, he was the same Ross. "Why are you always arguing with me?"

He loosened the clutch of his arms and turned her around to face him. He didn't let go. "I'm not arguing with you. I'm trying to help you."

"If you want to help me, then find me a Sharpie." Becca dragged an arm up and wiped away the tears that she didn't even have an interest in stopping. Nothing mattered now. Not even Ross seeing her cry. "Although I don't know who the authorities would notify once they identified me. My grandmother Bess has been dead for more than a decade. And my mother's been dead to me even longer. Who even knows if she's still alive. There's no one who will even care if I'm gone."

Ross brushed a hand across the side of her hair, curving his fingers gently behind her ear, then sweeping down to her shoulder and back to the embrace.

"I care," he said in a low and deliberate tone.

"Well, you don't count. You're coming with me. That warning was for you too." She sniffed back, and her nose felt as full and unruly as her emotions.

"I'm not going anywhere, Becca."

He sounded like he meant it. Becca wished she could have mustered even one one-hundredth of that certainty. But she couldn't.

She'd tried to leave Port Provident. She'd been in line for the last bus. But she couldn't say no to a Labrador she'd never met. Now they would all be paying the price.

"And Polly...I was supposed to take care of her. And Cookie. And the cats. We saved them, brought them here. But for what,

Ross? How is Mrs. McCaw ever going to know what happened to Polly?"

Becca slumped forward. She couldn't look at Polly in the corner, silently providing comfort to the frightened Cookie. She couldn't look at Ross in front of her, doing his best to provide the same.

"You're going to tell her, Becca." Ross' hands gently patted her back. He whispered a low shushing noise near her ear.

If she let the sob in her throat go, Becca knew she'd choke on everything welling up inside. All the clichés were about the smell of fear. They were wrong.

It was the taste of fear that filled Becca's senses—the raw bile in her throat, the thick feel of phlegm that prevented her from swallowing effectively, the dry furring of her tongue.

If she gave in, she would never come back from it. She knew it.

She would drown in her own fear before the water ever touched her.

"I can't." Becca forced out a whisper from between shock-parched lips.

"'When you go through deep waters, I will be with you'," Ross said, still close enough to her ear that she could hear him over the thrash of the storm outside and feel the tickle of his breath through dislodged strands of hair.

Becca pulled her face back from the cotton of Ross' shirt. A large spot of tears and terror was marked there in the center.

"You don't have to be my lifeguard, Ross. I'm not expecting that."

He stroked her ponytail slowly. "Not me. Those aren't my words. That's from the book of Isaiah. It's a promise from God."

"God doesn't make promises to me. Believe me." She wiggled a bit and tried to pull away. This was tough enough without Ross plugging God nonsense in there. "I just need that marker, Ross. Do you have one up here?"

Becca took a step backward and pushed on the cross of Ross' arms against her back. He dropped them to his side.

"In the kitchen drawer that's under the telephone," he said. She could hear the reluctance in his voice. She just couldn't tell what it was underscoring. Was he reluctant to admit the truth—that his Sunday School lessons weren't going to help them when the peak of the storm's fury hit?

Or was he reluctant to let her go?

She yanked the cap off the black marker, as the small but satisfying sound of the lid popping off released some of the pent up anger and fear she held inside.

"Either way, doesn't matter," she muttered.

How Ross heard her over the deafening roar just beyond the door baffled her. "What doesn't matter?"

Defiantly, Becca touched the tip of the marker to the inside of her forearm and began to write the chain of numbers. She scratched the dashes between the groupings with extra force.

Nine numbers, two dashes.

And come morning, it would probably represent the sum total of who she was.

"You. Me. I guess." She knew she was completely ineloquent, but that didn't matter either. "Any of this. What will be, will be. *Que será, será.*"

Becca held the marker out to Ross, the soft, inky tip pointed toward his own forearm—the same forearm that had tried so hard to brace her, to comfort her just moments before.

Ross took the marker from her and followed her lead. Becca was surprised to see how small his handwriting was, but she wasn't at all shocked by the precision with which he wrote, even on the stretchy surface of skin.

"This doesn't mean I'm giving up, Becca." He picked the cap up off the counter and snapped it back on the marker.

"You think I'm giving up?"

"That's not what I meant at all."

"Then what did you mean? Why are you acting like none of this concerns you?" She pointed at the nearby uncovered window. "You heard what the mayor said too. You can see what's going on out there. We're in a garage apartment, but look out there—the water is at the top of the garage doors all along your alley. How much longer until it's in here with us?"

He walked around her and stood near the window, surveying all the destruction below. The rain slapped at the window and made it rattle in the aluminum frame.

"Clearly I should have bought the Rugged Edition package for my truck," he said wryly.

Something inside of her broke, like the snapping of a twig. "I don't want to joke, Ross. I just want to know what to do."

He moved out of the kitchen, away from the window, before speaking.

"I don't know what to do, Becca. But I do know we're not going to fix it by arguing." He ran a hand through his hair and let out a deep breath. "Maybe you're right. Maybe I am. Maybe we're both saying the same thing in different ways. I honestly don't know. What I do know is that I saw hell in Iraq. I never thought I'd see it here at home, but if I look outside, that's what I see. It's a very different kind of hell, but it's just as overwhelming and scary and out of my own personal control as anything over there was. But I survived that—and I helped a lot of my patients survive, too. I just can't wrap my mind around losing *this* battle when I'm in my own backyard."

Maybe he *was* right.

Either way, Becca still felt like she could start trembling again at any minute. And if she began to shake again, lost in the storm of her own feelings and despair and fear, she didn't think anything would be able to make it stop.

Her limbs started to feel weighed down, like they were full of quicksand. Her eyes felt the same downward pull.

"I think I'm tired," Becca said. "Is it possible to sleep during a hurricane?"

"The adrenaline pop is wearing off. You can use the futon if you'd like. It's surprisingly comfortable. Cookie and I sit there when we watch TV."

Ross pointed at a blue cushion tossed over a wooden frame at the side of the living room.

Becca furrowed her forehead. "Is that blue suede?"

Ross cocked an eyebrow as he answered. "Maybe."

"Like blue, blue, blue suede futon?"

"Maaaaybe." He was clearly poking fun at himself.

It felt good to smile again, even just for a second. "Wait a minute. And Cookie is your hound dog?"

A little twinkle formed in his eye. Even in the dim of the candlelight, she could see his cocky grin and the accompanying mischief.

"Thank you. Thank you very much." Ross lifted his lip in a comical imitation of Elvis' distinct way of speaking.

Becca sank low onto the base plane of the futon as soon as she got near. Despite the humidity in the air and the stuffiness inside the garage apartment from not having electricity or air conditioning, the suede felt cool where it touched her skin.

"If only I had a peanut butter and banana sandwich right about now." She placed her head back against the blue tufting.

Ross came over and sat beside her. "Here, you can lean on me. I'm no hunka'-hunka' burning love, but I promise to wake you up if we need to move quickly. That way you can really get some rest without having to worry about keeping one eye open."

"But what about you? Don't you need some rest too?"

"Don't worry about me, Becca. I've slept with one eye open more times than I care to acknowledge." He gently drew her back into his arms and laid her head on his chest. Just as earlier, the simple contact calmed her.

There were no arguments—nor were there any expectations that his holding her meant something else. It was an uncomplicated gesture of support, an acknowledgment that they were in this together—whatever it wound up being.

Becca touched at the ink on her forearm.

"Get your rest, Becca. We're not going to need that. I promise. I don't know what else is to come tonight, but I won't let you down. The official motto of the United States Army is 'This we'll defend.' I haven't forgotten the commitment behind those words." He adjusted his position and leaned back slightly on the futon cushion so he could better support her. "Tonight, Becca, I'll defend you."

The way the small apartment shook and rattled and swayed scared Ross in a way he had never expected to feel again. He thought he'd left all that behind in another part of the world with another career. His thoughts strayed to Cookie, who'd finally seemed to settle down thanks to the support of a new, loyal friend and a familiar tennis ball.

Like the winds outside, his mind twisted and turned as the minutes stretched into hours.

And somehow, his mind landed on the most unexpected part of this whole day—Becca Collins in his arms.

Anyone would have done what he had this evening. You didn't just leave a person to feel hopeless and alone at one of the worst moments in their lives. The mayor's statement had turned to ice in his heart, too. But the instant he took in Becca's body language, he knew he could never show how he felt.

The candles burned low in the apartment, and the wind shrieked like a full cohort of banshees outside. It threw tree limbs and trash cans and anything not nailed down. The debris hit the walls of the house and glanced off the roof, stripping shingles and making everything shake.

Somehow, though, Becca slept through the chaos. Ross was glad. He and Becca definitely had their differences, but this was life-and-death. They'd shared a permanent marker together and gave quiet voice to deep fears.

What did that mean, exactly, though? Ross wasn't sure. He didn't see them just all of a sudden getting along simply because they'd shared some mac and cheese and a Sharpie. Once you left kindergarten, life wasn't like that.

When the water rolled back to the gulf and drained once more out to the bay, Becca Collins would still be strong-willed, impulsive, and prone to big ideas with little thought for how to actually accomplish them.

But if she hadn't been all of those things to begin with, one geriatric Labrador retriever, two kittens, and a porch-bound cat certainly would have lost their lives tonight.

Before Ross even had the opportunity to process all of his thoughts about Becca and everything they'd been through the last few hours, he became acutely aware of another thought.

Silence.

Abruptly, the wind had just stopped. The rain was no longer falling.

This must be the eye of the storm. Funny—he'd heard so many people reference it metaphorically. How strange to actually be *living* it.

Slowly, he adjusted Becca's position on the futon and eased out from his spot behind her. Polly's tail flapped on the floor as she took in the change of sound and Ross' movement.

Ross walked to the door and placed a cautious hand on the knob. He wasn't sure quite what he was expecting, but he knew he'd remember this moment forever. He knew what he'd see would stay with him, shape him, for the rest of his life.

He twisted the brass knob and tugged.

Stretched out before him was Port Provident. At least he thought it was. Everything seemed far more port than providential, though. Specifically, he thought it resembled a deep-water port.

Emphasis on water.

Water, water everywhere...nor any drop to drink.

He remembered the *Rime of the Ancient Mariner*. Verses slid through his mind, vestiges of English literature classes past. Sitting in those uncomfortable high school desks, fighting the urge to do as Shakespeare'd said—"to sleep, perchance to dream"—he never thought that one day he'd be living out a literary classic.

Well, not completely. At the moment, Ross completely identified with the mariner's struggles...but he refused to think of himself as ancient.

As he scanned left, then right, then stared at the watery, gray horizon as intently as he could, Ross felt the brush of fur first on one leg, then on the other. He stole a glance downward to see Polly standing on his left. Surprisingly, Cookie sat at attention next to Ross's right leg. He still clutched the tennis ball in his mouth. It had turned to a drooly, green sphere of fuzz that was practically unrecognizable under all the wet.

Much like Port Provident itself.

Ross leaned down and gave Cookie a hearty scratch behind the ears, then repeated the gesture behind Polly's ears.

As they stood there in a companionable, stunned silence, Ross saw an aluminum boat puttering down the water that covered the alley. Judging by the water line on his garage and those of his neighbors, Ross estimated the surge here to be more than ten feet deep. Probably closer to eleven. Any one-story homes in the area would be complete losses.

The captain of the small boat maneuvered as best he could, angling as close to Ross' staircase as possible. Where once he would have stood a full story below Ross' front door, now he was only about three stairs below the small porch at the top of the stairs.

"Dr. Reeder?"

Ross' curiosity was piqued. He couldn't imagine someone leaving their home in the middle of all this, much less leaving for *him*.

"How can I help you?"

The man was covered, head to toe, in a heavy-duty blue rain suit. The hood was tightened down as much as possible, leaving only a small circle of eyes, nose, and mouth visible amidst a frame of dark skin.

"I'm Lieutenant Cal Perkins of the Port Provident Police Department. Rigo Vasquez said I'd find you here."

"I'm pretty sure I don't have any outstanding warrants. And this really isn't subpoena-serving weather, so…" Ross made sure his words were punctuated with a smile.

"No, sir, it's not. I'm part of the team working at the shelter of last resort at Port Provident High School. We have a problem, and I need your help. I need you to come with me right now—we don't have much time before this eye passes."

Ross was at a complete loss. A police officer at a shelter had a pressing need for his help?

"I'm always happy to help, sir, but I'm afraid I don't understand."

Lieutenant Perkins braced the boat against one of the pilings that held up the staircase. "We have a large number of animals that have been brought in. And with the eye of the storm, we're expecting more as the people who are able to do so move from where they've been staying to the protection of the shelter."

"I thought you weren't taking animals at the high school. Becca Collins from the Port Provident Animal Shelter was turned away earlier today because she had a Labrador with her."

The man shook his head. "Ideally, we wouldn't. But right before the city shut down rescues because things had gotten too dangerous, we were overwhelmed by last-minute refugees. We couldn't send them back because of the conditions. So, we had to take them all—and their dogs, cats, guinea pigs...and more."

"I see." Ross wanted to help, but he hesitated. He had obligations already. Especially to one animal in particular. He wouldn't leave Cookie to face the second half of this storm alone. "But I have animals of my own here. I can't leave them behind."

The officer surveyed the space in the boat. "How many?"

"Two Labradors, three cats, me, and Becca Collins."

"I think we've got enough room. But I need you to hurry."

A sense of cold, numb steel overwhelmed Ross' senses. He wasn't sure about how he felt about leaving his house to ride in a boat to the high school when the storm could sweep back to full-force at any minute. He didn't have any expectations of how long Hope's eye should last.

"Dr. Reeder, we need to go."

There were probably rules about disobeying a direct request from a law enforcement officer in the middle of a natural disaster, Ross figured. It didn't matter how he felt about it. Port Provident needed him—and Becca.

"Let me go get Becca and the animals. We'll be right out."

Ross ducked back inside and made a straight line for the futon. He gently shook Becca's shoulder. "Becca, the eye of the storm is here. Port Provident PD sent a boat for us, and the dogs and the cats. They need us to come to the shelter at the high school. We have to leave right now."

Her eyes parted slowly. "What? Leave? We can't. Ross—I can't go out in the middle of a hurricane. We'll die."

"It's the eye of the storm, Becca. It's completely calm out there right now. There's no wind, no rain. We'll be fine." He swallowed against the words. He felt like he was lying to Becca, even though he knew he really wasn't. Either way, he didn't have a choice. "But we have to go right now. There's a uniformed police officer waiting on us. Can you help me gather up the cats?"

She stood and started walking toward the bedroom. "I think they went under the bed. I'll get them. Grab my backpack and the food for Polly."

Ross picked up another backpack from a closet near the door and stuffed a few T-shirts and a pair of shorts from his laundry pile in there. They were dirty, but at this point, it didn't matter. He reached in the drawer to the left of the telephone and pulled out a small folder of important papers he didn't want to leave behind. The dogs followed closely—their instinct told them not to get too far away.

Becca came back, three cats in her arms.

"I got the biggest backpack I could find. They're not going to like this, but let's put them in here." Ross held the main pouch open. Becca placed the squirming balls of fur gently on top of the wadded-up laundry. Ross pulled the double zippers together but left a gap of about an inch at the very top for air.

"Here's yours." He gestured toward where he'd set her blue nylon bag on the counter.

They each put the straps of their respective bags over their shoulders. Ross looked at Becca with a steady gaze. He could see the tension in her face. Her lips were set in a thin line, and her eyes darted around the room.

"Come on Polly. Come on Cookie—don't forget your tennis ball." He whistled as he stepped through the door that he'd forgotten to shut behind him earlier. "Here we go."

Becca closed the door behind them without saying a word. "You want to lock it?"

Ross surveyed the watery apocalypse all around them. "Nah. What's the point?"

~

Ross and the officer kept joking about how the ark seemed larger when they read about it in the Bible, but otherwise, they'd come two by two —with an extra cat for good measure.

Becca did not understand how they could joke at a time like this. All she felt was a deep sense of dread in the pit of her stomach, which growled uneasily. It had been a long time since the mac and cheese.

It seemed like even longer since she'd been dry and safe. She decided it was better to close her eyes and try her best to keep her thoughts clear.

"Wow, look at that." Ross' voice was filled with disbelief.

Becca didn't want to look at anything—that would have meant opening her eyes, and opening her eyes meant filling her senses with more to fear—but Ross gave an insistent tap on her shoulder.

Skeptically, she cocked her head and opened her left eye into a lopsided squint.

"Hmm?" The wordless syllable was all she could articulate.

"The sky. Look at it. That's incredible. I've never seen anything like it." His hand rested on her shoulder. "You'll want to remember this moment."

Becca opened both eyes fully.

In a matter of minutes, the sky had transformed from the solid mass of clouds that had filled it for hours on end. Now it sparkled, a clear teal that ran from the line of the horizon all the way to the outer limits of the heavens, it seemed.

"I've only seen that color in photos of tropical water. Never in the sky."

Ross shook his head, a smile filling all the corners and curves of his face. "Me neither. I never imagined a sky could look like this."

Lieutenant Perkins chimed in. "We haven't had a major hurricane here in Port Provident for decades. But I've been around for some smaller storms—a few Category Ones and the like. The sky in the eye is always incredible. And once the storm moves through, we usually have Caribbean-like water. But yeah, I've never seen it quite like this. My Granny would have loved to see this. She loved sitting on her porch watching God paint the heavens, as she put it."

A sudden memory of Bess gripped Becca. They'd gone for the weekend to a lake when she was eight or nine. It was the only vacation she ever took as a child. They stood, hand-in-hand, on the lake shore and watched the sunset reflect down, down, down into the water. All around the setting sun were stripes of red and orange and colors she'd never seen before—not even in the largest crayon boxes.

Bess had sighed at the sight. "The Bible says the heavens declare the glory of God. And I guess they do, Rebecca. I guess they do," she said.

Bess believed in God and had tried to pass that to Becca. Even so, Becca couldn't place why that memory and that quote, of all things, gripped her heart so tightly right now.

It was probably all that ark talk from earlier. She tried to push it out of her mind and level-set her thinking. If there really was some glorious, sky-painting, all-caring God, she wouldn't be sitting in a small boat with opinionated Ross Reeder, two wet dogs, and a backpack full of cats. She wouldn't have had to identify herself with a marker on her forearm.

And she wouldn't have gone to sleep believing she would never wake up again.

As they docked at what had once been the steps to the door of Port Provident High School, a flock of more than twenty seagulls circled overhead. Clouds were pushing into view once again. Clearly, the passage of the eye was almost complete. They needed to get inside and get settled—quickly. As Ross reached out his hand to help Becca out of the boat, the wind whipped across the surface of the standing water, putting an exclamation point on Becca's sense of urgency.

"I need to secure the boat," Lieutenant Perkins said, raising his voice slightly to be heard above the sounds of the hurricane rolling back in. "Go inside and ask for Officer Tafoya. She'll be able to show you where you need to go."

Ross picked up the backpack of cats and helped a skeptical Polly and Cookie splash toward the door.

Becca hesitated. She turned her head to look over her shoulder.

"You coming, Becca?" Ross asked.

"Yeah," she said and put one wet foot in front of the other.

She'd wanted to see one last streak of teal. In truth, she'd wanted to hold on to that crystal-clear memory of her darling Bess just a little longer, even though she couldn't say precisely why.

5

The team from Port Provident PD that had been doing their best to loosely manage the chaos inside of Port Provident High School had tried to corral all the dogs into one math classroom and all the cats in another. Unfortunately, neither species was particularly impressed by their pre-calculus surroundings.

The power generated off the backup generator wasn't doing much to keep the rooms adequately lit, and the smell of fear and tinkle and fur was obnoxious. Becca had spent most of her adult life in an animal shelter, and the situation she currently surveyed made her nose twitch.

"This is not going to work," Ross said after letting out a low whistle.

"Not at all." Becca had to raise her voice to be heard over the steady stream of yapping, howling and whining. "There's way too much stress and unhappiness here. We need a better place to stage this. Larger, more open, more light, and the ability for owners to remain with their pets if they choose."

"Well, we're using the band hall to stage supplies, and the cafeteria and gym are where all the people are sheltering," Officer Tafoya said, backing away from the furry, maddening crowd.

Becca thought for a moment. "Library," she said—at the same moment Ross came to an identical conclusion.

"Jinx?" He laughed. "I know we're in a high school, but we don't have to pinky swear or anything, right?"

"Pretty sure I've never pinky-sworn in my whole life. I didn't go to one of those kind of high schools."

"I didn't either, really. I went to DOD schools on bases all over the place. But I've got three sisters. I've seen my fair share of jinxes and pinky swears. It's just protocol."

Ross tried to keep a straight face, but couldn't. Watching the smile on his face added a bit of levity to the crazy situation they found themselves in. Too bad there wasn't a way to get these dogs and cats—and that ferret in the corner—to laugh along with them.

"I don't think anyone is using the library," Officer Tafoya said. "But I'm not sure about animals around the books and equipment in there."

Becca felt pretty strongly about this one and already had mapped out a plan in her mind. "I understand the concerns. But we already have one dog with us who suffers from combat-induced PTSD, and we have no way of knowing the individual health issues of these other animals. It's our responsibility to make sure that we take care of them as best we can right now, and the first step in that is trying to minimize the stress in their environment. There's no way we're going to eliminate all of that in the middle of a hurricane, but we need to do what we can. Dr. Reeder and I are both professionals in this area. I'm asking you and the other people in charge here to please trust us."

Ross nodded in agreement. "We'll do our best to control the situation, but we need to move to the library."

He said in one sentence what it had taken Becca several to articulate. That was typical of all their interactions. His voice held more than a hint of "military officer" in it, and Officer Tafoya shrugged.

"Go do what you've gotta do. I'm turning this problem over to you —and gladly so. I work vice, not animal control."

Officer Tafoya headed in the direction of the cafeteria, leaving

Becca and Ross in the hallway with the animals they'd brought in the boat. The howling continued on the other side of the doors to the math classrooms.

"Here's what I'm thinking—if we can block off the aisles, we can put animals of similar temperaments together since we're not going to find crates or cages here." Becca started mapping out the arrangement with her hands.

"I agree with you. Having a free-for-all in these rooms isn't working."

Becca continued. "Another thing—potty. Obviously, we can't take them outside, but they can't just go wherever. Talk about a territory-marking mess."

"Right. Hey, don't they have a daycare program in here for the teen moms in the district?"

A light clicked on in Becca's head, and her mind was flooded with big ideas. "Yes, they do. Diapers. We can carpet a back corner with diapers and encourage the dogs to use that as an indoor yard. And I bet they have some pack-and-play type things or cribs in there. We can use those for some groups of animals."

"Perfect." That easy smile found its way to Ross' face again, and Becca surprised herself by acknowledging how much she enjoyed seeing it. "Auto shop might have kitty litter for soaking up spills."

"Great idea. I'll go to the nursery. You go to the auto shop. Check and see if there are any crates and anything we could use as leashes, too. I'll meet you back in the library as soon as possible."

Ross gave her a thumbs up and then started down the hall, Cookie trailing behind him. Abruptly, he stopped and turned around.

"What?" Becca asked.

"The cats." He jogged back a few paces and picked up the backpack of cats and put it back over his shoulders. "Cookie and I will see you ladies in a few minutes."

Polly followed Becca to the T at the end of the hall. Becca studied the sign with arrows, pointing out the direction of various areas of the school. It looked like they needed to go left in order to be on the right track to the Child Life Center.

By following the signs, Becca and Polly made it through the dim halls with a minimum of wrong turns. She wished the signs on Ross were just as easy to read.

Becca had spent the better part of the last two years thinking only negative thoughts about Ross Reeder. She couldn't even think of any neutral thoughts she'd had about him. There definitely had not been any positive ones.

Until today.

She'd seen a new side—or two...or three—to him. Plus she couldn't believe how the thought of his smile had taken up a seemingly permanent residence in her mind. She couldn't shake the image.

It was better than thinking about that snake in the water earlier, and all the memories that had brought back.

Ok, it was *a lot* better.

But she still couldn't wrap her mind around anything about the veterinarian being stuck in her head on repeat. What a day it had been. First the hurricane, and now a seismic shift in how she viewed Ross. It was like a chain reaction of natural disasters in her life.

Except she was no longer sure that she considered Ross a natural disaster.

Becca cracked open the door to the Child Life Center. Polly stuck her nose in front of Becca's leg, wordlessly telling Becca that she would be doing a quick reconnaissance mission before Becca would be allowed to enter.

Through all the uncertainty of today, Polly had been a sweetheart—one of the best dogs Becca had ever known. She took her change in guardianship in stride, then provided steady companionship to Cookie at the crate, and now put her best paw forward at protecting Becca.

Becca held the door open a little wider for Polly to more easily pass through and realized that when all this was over, she'd miss having Polly by her side as much as she'd miss catching glimpses of Ross' smile.

Now, if that wasn't the sign of a world turned upside-down, Becca didn't know what a more obvious signal would be.

Polly wagged her tail, waving Becca inside the large nursery area.

Even with the bare minimum of lights in here, Becca could see this had been a cheerful place. Smiles and love were evident. Primary colors, teddy bears—and a tall bookshelf stacked full of diapers. Jackpot.

The perimeter of the room was lined with cribs and portable playpens, just as Becca had hoped. She quickly got to work dismantling the pack-and-plays, folding them up and stacking them in a crib. Once that was done, she piled diapers in another one. To that crib, she added bowls from a play kitchen that could be used for water dishes and several warehouse-store-sized boxes of cereal and fish-shaped crackers. They weren't ideal animal nutrition by a long shot, but they would do for the few hours she had to keep this operation running. She might even eat some herself.

Becca also found some long lengths of brightly-colored grosgrain ribbon that could be tied to collars to use as leashes, if necessary, and a set of interlocking plastic walls that could be reassembled to shape a tower that the cats might take to. She piled as much bedding as she could find on top and began to pull the crib toward the door.

Heavy and awkward didn't even begin to describe the slow trip with the crib, but Becca managed to get the awkward rectangle in the hallway. She repeated the process with the crib full of pack-and-plays. An officer walked by as she was closing the door to the Child Life Center, and Becca flagged him down.

They slowly pushed the cribs together through the corridors until they reached the library in the center of the building.

Ross was already hard at work, stacking tables and chairs and wrapping the legs with paper from several large rolls of construction paper he appeared to have taken out of the teachers' supply room. He fastened the paper tightly with tape and arranged everything into a series of corrals and mazes. He quickly unpacked the cribs Becca had stocked and moved.

In just over half an hour, the entire library had been transformed. The makeshift animal shelter was ready for business.

"Not bad, Collins." Ross put his arm around Becca's shoulder and gave it a gentle squeeze. "Not bad at all."

This time, the easy, relaxed smile that appeared was on Becca's face, and she knew it. She felt pride in what they'd pulled together against some pretty steep odds. She felt grateful for the opportunity to do work that she knew—real work—and take her mind off the storm raging outside.

And, most surprisingly of all, Becca realized she felt no sense of protest at being in Ross' arms once again.

Owners had been reunited with pets in designated sections in the library. Bowls were full of cereal and water. An area layered with diapers in the back corner had been selected as the official potty area, and boxes of kitty litter were stationed nearby. Some animals had been placed in barricaded areas, and others passed the time in pack-and-plays and cribs. A few teenagers and pre-teens taking refuge in the school had been brought in to play with the animals and walk them to the potty and food areas. In all, it had taken a little more than an hour to restore order to chaos and to make Port Provident's animals as comfortable and settled as they could be.

Ross sat in a tall, blue plastic chair behind the library's circulation desk. Cookie had found a cubby near Ross' feet where he felt content. Periodically, he would adjust the position of the tennis ball in his mouth, but he never fully let it go.

The three cats Ross and Becca had rescued stayed together in one of the pack-and-plays that Ross moved behind the desk so he could keep an eye on them.

He watched as Becca walked around, clipboard in hand, making notes and taking inventory of the animals. Some had their owners with them—others had been brought in by the Port Provident Police Department or Beach Patrol during the rescues and searches earlier in the storm. The only information they would have to try and reunite dogs with owners would be what Becca could find on the dogs themselves.

"One of the officers came in about fifteen minutes ago and told me that the storm is almost completely across Provident Island," Ross said, as Becca came back to the circulation desk.

"About time," she replied. "This has been the longest day ever."

"It sure seems like it. But what are we going to do with all these animals? They're going to clear out the shelter in a few hours and half of these guys were brought here without owners."

Becca placed the clipboard on the desk.

"I know. I expect there will be some damage to the Port Provident Animal Shelter, but I guess it's the best bet. Remember, my car is in the parking lot here. Maybe if it still runs, I can get over there and do some quick cleaning up and then we can transport them over there. I'd call some shelters in Houston, but I don't guess we have phone service right now. As soon as we do, though, I'll call some shelter directors I know and see what help they can offer."

There were a lot of unanswered questions in Becca's statement, but Ross had to agree. It was probably the best plan they could put together at this point. The clock was ticking down until they got evicted from their temporary shelter they'd put together here in the library.

"Ok, we'll call that our plan of record, Becca." He looked straight into her eyes. They were equal parts tired and troubled. "What's wrong?"

She sighed and leaned over, letting her elbows rest on the desktop and her chin rest on her curled fists.

"Just thinking about today. I never in a million years would have dreamed this is what going through a hurricane would be like. I grew up in a pretty tough neighborhood—I saw people die when I was in elementary school. And I've been through a lot in my life. But I don't think I truly ever thought *I'd* die like I did earlier." She raised her eyes, looking at him through the fringe of her eyelashes. "Thank you for being there for me tonight. You weren't scared. I mean, I feel pretty silly now just thinking about it."

She let out another deep breath, and Ross could feel the weight she was carrying on her shoulders.

"That's not exactly true."

"What's not?"

"Saying I wasn't scared. I was pretty close to terrified at a few points. Like you, I've seen a thing or two in my life also. But this was something else—nowhere to run if the water came pouring in. Nowhere to hide if the roof got ripped off. I barely had a Plan A. I definitely didn't have a Plan B. And, I always operate with a Plan B."

The disdain in Becca's laugh surprised him a bit. "Ha. Tell me—why do you hate the idea for the new shelter so much?"

Ross was surprised they'd spent as much time together in close quarters as they had today and not really even touched on the subject. But apparently, the time was now. They'd built some trust between them today. He owed it to her—and to himself—to not disrespect it.

"I don't hate the concept, Becca."

"Pooh. You do too."

He could have sworn she rolled her eyes, but he wasn't one-hundred-percent sure. His first urge was to answer with "do not." But since he hadn't been four years old in a long time, he figured that wasn't the appropriate response.

"No, honestly, I don't. I just don't think you can afford it. Your main annual fundraiser is The Paw Ball at Provident Mardi Gras, and the amount of money it brings in has declined for the last two years. Your grants coordinator left, so you've got a decrease in revenue in that area too."

She bit her lower lip. "I know. But we were trying to add another fundraiser at the holidays and maybe something tourist-related in the summer. I know money's slow right now, but I keep getting the feedback that no one wants to be a part of what we're doing because they assume we're not worth getting involved with since our facilities are old. The message we're sending to potential donors and volunteers is that we're doing something wrong. Our facilities look like a medieval dungeon compared to what's just up the road in Houston. The money is going up there. I have to do something to instill confidence in people that we're a worthwhile organization. The cliché is true—you never get a second chance to make a first impression. And the first impression that my shelter makes doesn't inspire people to get on board."

Ross could feel the emotion in her words. She spoke passionately and articulated her thoughts strongly.

"You've never spoken like this in board meetings, Becca. Why not?"

She raised a shoulder and lowered it. "Same basic reason, I guess. I don't want to highlight our issues to the board. I don't want to make us look worse than we already are."

"But we need to know. I look at the numbers—I'm an analytical, rational guy. But I don't know what all these people are saying if you don't tell me—or the rest of the board. We should all be on the same team."

"I never thought it would matter to you," she said. "You had your mind made up the first time we started discussing this a year ago."

"That's not accurate, Becca. I looked at what I had available to me —the accounting reports and projections for the year ahead and the annual report and such—and I used it to make an informed decision."

She stood up straight. "But when was the last time you took a tour of the facilities and spent time with us outside of the boardroom?"

Becca had him there. The truth was he didn't want to spend any more time around her than necessary—he experienced enough tension and arguing at the board meetings to last him for the full four weeks between each session. "I don't remember."

"When we get out of here today, I'd be happy to give you a tour."

"Um, Becca?" Ross spoke warily. "I'm not sure you'd be putting your best foot forward today."

"Um, Ross…" she drummed her fingers on the desk for emphasis. "It will be a little wetter, but other than that, trust me, it's probably not going to matter much."

Ross wasn't sure whether to laugh or to agree with her. Maybe she was exaggerating. Maybe she was right.

Or maybe this one was all on him. Maybe he'd been making assumptions and calling them facts.

Maybe he'd been wrong about more than just what was in the best interests of the Port Provident Animal Shelter.

Maybe he'd been wrong about Becca Collins and it was taking a hurricane named Hope to wash away the ideas he'd held as truth for years.

Becca held her breath as Ross put the key in the ignition of her old car. As surprising as the last day had been, the speed with which the water receded once the storm had passed was something Becca could never have imagined. She figured it would be days for the water to recede to where the streets of Port Provident no longer resembled the canals of Venice.

But here they were, at the far corner of the Port Provident High School parking lot, holding a collective breath to see whether they'd be driving to the animal shelter to check the damage or taking a long, pet-laden walk back to Ross' clinic and garage apartment to come up with alternative transportation ideas.

A mechanical sputtering sound bloomed into a grumble. The little hatchback shook and swaggled and then came fully to life.

"Oh, my gosh, Ross! It's not dead! I can't believe this. I saw the water in this parking lot. I don't even know what to say."

Becca felt short of breath from the dizzying excitement of a running car, a metallic survivor.

"Thank you is probably the right place to start," Ross said.

"All you did was turn the key. You didn't do this."

He raised an eyebrow and leaned down under the dashboard to pull the lever which would pop the car's hood. "Not me. God. There's no way this car starts without a miracle."

Ross looked at the surrounding neighborhood as he walked to the front bumper and peered inside. "There's no way this town rebuilds without a miracle. I can't even imagine what's to come."

She felt awkward with his talk about God and miracles. Why couldn't he just be happy about their good luck? Why did he always have to have a reason? And why did it always seem to have to be about God?

If there was a God, He had better things to do than worry about flooded cars. Like maybe, you know, little girls locked in closets... But since she knew firsthand that He didn't do anything about little girls in closets, she knew he didn't give a lick of care about water in cars.

For someone who prided himself on being as practical as Ross Reeder did, it actually disappointed Becca to see him quote crazy fairytales like they were absolute truth. But as soon as they drove away from the high school, she'd be just a short ride away from her home and business. And a short ride away from putting Ross Reeder back in a corner of her life.

Of course, she was grateful that she had been given the opportunity to learn more about Ross and to have conversations with him that didn't reek of rancor. That would probably pay dividends for their work together on the board in the years to come. But when it was all said and done, she would be glad to go back to primarily having the company of animals.

They didn't talk nonsense. They didn't frustrate her. And they most certainly didn't make her think of being wrapped in their arms.

It took more than forty minutes to make a drive that would have usually taken ten. They stopped several times to clear debris out of the street, and more than once had to turn around and find a new route when the way was blocked entirely.

"It looks like a war zone," Becca said softly as they turned on what had been one of Port Provident's main streets.

Ross clenched his jaw.

"I'm sorry, I guess you've seen real war zones. This probably doesn't look like one at all." Becca corrected her observation.

Ross dodged a refrigerator in the middle of the road, then made a left turn that would take them straight to the animal shelter—hopefully.

"No offense taken. It's probably the best way to describe this. I just can't take it all in. I'm not sure there's a palm frond still attached to a tree trunk anywhere on this island. And the boats on the curbs, the trash in the yards, the patio furniture everywhere. I am glad I'm not in charge here. I wouldn't even know what to do first."

All the power lines alongside Harborview Drive had been pulled down. Black cable lay broken in ominous puddles and twists down the entire length of the road. Nothing along Harborview looked anything like it had the last time she'd driven this way—which was only a little more than twenty-four hours ago.

It scared her to think how much change the water and wind had probably brought to the animal shelter. Becca lowered her head into her hands. She just couldn't take any more in.

Ross gave her shoulder a quick squeeze. "It's going to be okay."

"I'm not so sure. There's no denying the reality when you look all around." Her interlaced fingers muffled her words.

"Here we are." The car swayed around a turn as Ross announced they'd reached their destination. "You want to look?"

"No."

"That's not going to change anything, Becca. The storm's in the past. You've got to accept the reality. That way you can move forward."

"Could you just drop me off at the bus station instead?" The words came out before she really thought them through. But, it had worked out once before. Now that she thought of it, that wasn't a terrible idea. Maybe this whole storm was a sign she needed a fresh start again.

"No." Ross answered without hesitation. "There aren't any buses left on the island. And why would you run away?"

She didn't look up, just freed a hand and gestured randomly. "Yeah. I see lots of reasons to stay."

"Your hands are covering your eyes. You can't see anything." She felt the car come to a stop. "Besides, there are five reasons in the backseat, about twenty back at the high school library, and…well, one in the front seat."

Becca pulled herself back to an upright position. "You?"

He shrugged. "Well, maybe. I'd hate to see you run off to some other dot on a map right after we finally become friends. I honestly don't have that many people I really consider friends here in Port Provident. Lots of acquaintances. Not as many friends."

She hadn't really thought of Ross as a friend. But maybe he was right. If she was honest, she didn't have a long list of people she could truly call on in a pinch, either. Ross had certainly proven himself to make the short list there—and she'd never have dreamed that after the clash at their last board meeting.

"Are you ready to go inside?" He turned off the car.

"I don't think so. But I don't think it matters. I guess I have to do it, regardless, right?'

He got out, then opened the back door and put a leash on Cookie and another on Polly, then once again, put on the cat-filled backpack. "Yeah, you do. But we're going to go together. All seven of us. You won't be alone."

She placed a reluctant hand on the door and let herself out of the car as Ross took care of the animals. "You and Cookie and Polly, I trust. I'm just not sure about the level of support that's going to come from those cats."

"Me neither. But they're practically family now." Ross handed Becca Polly's leash. "Come on, let's go."

Becca's hand moved as though the lock were made of quicksand. She clumsily fumbled the key into the hole and then turned it so slowly as to almost not move it at all. When the door finally swung open, she held her breath—but not, she realized, because of trepidation. She held it because of the smell inside.

"Wow, you can clearly see the water line up there." Ross pointed less than a foot down from the top of the twelve-foot ceiling, where a gold-colored line squiggled all the way around the room.

A vise grip squeezed the lifeblood out of Becca's heart. She looked down at her arm, still bearing the numbers she'd scrawled on it in permanent marker at the height of the storm. "If the animals or I had stayed, we'd all be dead. No question about it."

"I can't even imagine what the surge was like when the water pushing in from the Gulf met the water here along the harbor."

The water still stood almost to a depth of mid-calf inside the building. It smelled of sewage and dead marine life and slime and things she couldn't even begin to place. Fuzzy brown and orange and red stuff she couldn't identify floated on the surface of the water everywhere.

"Is that wet dog food?" As Ross asked the question, Cookie pushed at some with his nose and gave it a sniff, then turned his head the other way.

"I think it is. But even Cookie knows how gross this mess is."

Becca sloshed around the center, checking out the front desk, the cat area, and the dog area. Everything had been completely submerged.

"It's all ruined," she said simply. A tear rolled out of the corner of her eye and down the curve of her cheek. She felt powerless to stop it. In fact, it felt futile to even think about stopping it.

What was one more drop of saltwater in the face of all this?

"I'm sorry, Becca. I don't know what else to say." Ross looked as stunned as Becca felt on the inside. At least she knew her mind wasn't exaggerating the trauma. Ross shared it with her. And something about that made it hurt a little less inside.

Maybe always flying solo and not inviting people into her space hadn't saved her from hurt over the years, as she'd always assumed. It was something to think about. Just not right now. Right now, she had to survey the one area she'd left for last.

"Your apartment's at the back, right, Becca?" Ross and Cookie stepped around a tumbled stack of cages.

She nodded. "It is. I guess there's no point in wasting more time out here. This isn't going to be a solution for housing those dogs and cats back at the high school."

Ross stepped out of Becca's path. "Lead the way."

With Polly half-swimming, half-trotting gingerly behind her, they navigated the main hallway that crossed the back of the building until they all came to the door at the end. "Here we go."

Her hand felt more steady as she unlocked this doorknob. Was there less fear now because she'd already resigned herself to her fate?

She turned the knob, then gave the door a shove.

It was everything she'd feared. The couch had overturned, and a spotty white film covered the cushions. Nothing was where she'd left it.

"Hold Polly," was all she said to Ross. She handed off the leash, then wandered around the small apartment with a detached sense of determination. She needed to see it all—even if she couldn't understand it.

The refrigerator had dumped on its side, and the door had somehow propped open, dumping all the contents to float in the water among pots and pans and other kitchen items. Becca crossed over to the side of the apartment where her bedroom and bathroom were. More of the same greeted her.

She heard splashing behind her. Ross and the dogs kept a respectful distance, but she knew they were witnesses to one of the lowest moments of her life, too.

Slowly, Becca turned around. "I came here with nothing. I guess I'm right back where I started."

Raising her gaze to look straight at Ross freed the tears that had begun to collect again in her eyes. He closed the distance between them with two splashing steps. Without hesitation, he wrapped her again in his arms.

She leaned into his chest, feeling like a stick of butter conforming against him. She pushed all the thoughts of her past and their past out of her head. None of it mattered now. None of it meant anything. Everything she knew to be true had just been washed away and destroyed in the last twenty-four hours.

Everything she'd worked for.

Everything she'd become.

She buried her head in Ross' shoulder and didn't care that he'd hear her crying. She didn't care that he'd see her broken—again. She only cared that Ross wouldn't let her fall if her legs suddenly went out from under her.

He raised one hand and gently stroked the curve of her hair from the crown to the place where the elastic held her ponytail in place.

Once, twice, three times. Becca felt lost in the gentle rhythm. When Ross' hand continued on the path and feathered across her cheek, it seemed like a fluid part of the process. He tucked a finger under her chin and pressed her face upward.

"Becca, look at me," he said softly.

She did. And in his eyes, she saw an ocean of concern greater even than the sea that had just flooded over their island. Not since Bess' death had Becca seen a look of care like this, meant for her.

He moved his finger from under her chin and used the soft pad of his thumb to wipe away the streams of salt water flowing down her face. The look in his eyes shifted subtly to something more intense. Inch by inch, his head moved a little lower, matching the angle of the tilt of her own head.

Inside, Becca felt a warmth overtake her. She no longer noticed how cold her feet were, standing in the murky water.

Ross stroked back a few wisps of hair from her face and pressed his lips gently in the middle of her forehead. The contact was soft, but there was no mistaking it. She didn't move except to close her eyes and just take in the feeling of the moment. There was too much heartbreak and destruction around her.

She wanted to focus on something that was good. Even if it was Ross. Even if she couldn't explain to herself how she felt about it.

He pulled back. She felt the damp of the humidity in the air paste over the two streaks where his lips had been. The contrast of warm-on-cool brought her back to reality, if reluctantly.

"We'll sort it all out, Becca. You can stay with me until there's a better plan. We'll figure something out for the animals. We're in this together now, you and me."

Together.

After a lifetime spent fending for herself, Becca barely believed that a destructive hurricane could be the thing that would bring her together with someone.

But for the first time in her life, she had to admit she'd rather not go through what was to come alone. And as she felt the warm memory of a gentle kiss that came with no strings or demands or expectations, Becca had to admit that maybe Ross Reeder was just what she needed to bring some balance to her life in the unbalanced days ahead.

6

*R*oss disassembled kennels and crates from his veterinary office, then hauled them up to the garage apartment for what seemed like hours. The vet clinic was in bad shape, but he figured out that the crates and kennels would just require a little TLC. He didn't like the fact that he had to set everything up on the porch that ran the length of the back of the garage apartment, but it was the best option he had available right now. In the morning, he would try and find the city's command center and see if there was a better space to utilize. For now, he could at least guarantee that all the animals that were still in the library of Port Provident High School would have food, water, and safety.

He looked up at the sky as he arranged the last kennel in place. There wasn't even a smudge of gray cloud above. No lingering rain. No forceful winds. Just a gentle breeze and some birds circling in the air.

It was as though yesterday had never happened, as though the middle-of-the-night boat ride to outrun the eye of the storm was only a figment of his imagination.

But that wasn't true at all. Because not only had Hurricane Hope happened, but he'd totally upended everything even further by kissing Becca Collins in the hallway at her waterlogged apartment.

What had he been thinking?

He'd like to dismiss the whole incident and say he just wasn't thinking or it was a reaction to stress. But he knew that wasn't the case at all. He wasn't the type to lie to himself, and he wasn't going to start now.

If he couldn't write it off as some crazy, misguided mistake, then that meant only one thing.

He'd wanted to kiss Becca.

The really honest truth was that he'd made a quick change of plans and instead of a full kiss, he'd forced himself to just drop one on her forehead. That way, if she asked, he could explain it away as friendly comfort.

But there was nothing friendly or comfortable about how he felt right now. When the last dog and cat were safely in this very temporary housing situation on his back deck, and he went inside his apartment for the night, what would he say to Becca? Was he supposed to pretend like nothing had happened?

Ross couldn't remember the last time he was without a Plan B.

Two yellow-and-red fifteen-passenger vans from Beach Patrol pulled up in the driveway downstairs. Dusk was falling, and there would be a curfew in Port Provident tonight, so time was of the essence. Ross had been able to get in a message to Rigo Vasquez through some other Port Provident PD officers about assistance. Vasquez had a few of the folks in his command pick up Becca earlier and arrange transport for all the animals that had still been in the library.

Dogs on leashes, cats in crates, three ferrets, two guinea pigs, and an old aquarium full of hamsters steadily made their way to the deck.

"Hamsters?" Ross said. "There were no hamsters in the library."

"We found them while we were doing welfare checks in the Texas Heroes neighborhood. The guinea pigs, too. I'm not sure where the ferrets came from." A younger Beach Patrol officer placed the last dog in one of the kennels, then closed the wire grid door.

"Okay. I might have some bedding for them in my upstairs supply room in the clinic. I know I have two rodent water bottles in there."

"We wrote down all the information we had on the animals we collected today and gave it to Becca," he said.

"Great. Thanks for all the help. If you see Chief Vasquez, tell him I'm going to need to find someone to talk to about getting a more permanent place to settle these animals tomorrow. My clinic is a mess, and the animal shelter is a total loss right now."

Just talking about the animal shelter made Ross' mind flashback to the feel of Becca's skin when he brushed his lips against her forehead. He was about to have to go inside and face her. And yet, he still didn't have a plan.

After the last of Beach Patrol drove away, Ross stalled on the deck, opening each kennel to check water and food and give each animal a pat behind the ears. The light in the sky faded to pitch black. With the power grid down, there were no street lights. There were no glowing windows in any of the neighboring houses. The curfew ensured that no one was outside, no cars were driving down the debris-laden streets.

In short, Ross felt utterly disconnected from the world on the porch. If he closed his eyes, he could imagine that he was alone on the island—except for the sniffing and panting and occasional high-pitched whimpering that surrounded him on the deck.

And the knowledge that Becca was just on the other side of the door.

Becca had fed the dogs, settled the cats and generally done everything she figured she could accomplish in a strange house with only candlelight to see by. It looked like dinner tonight would be a stack of un-cooked Pop-Tarts. To say that Ross' pantry was "bachelor chic" felt like an understatement. And since she knew he'd initially planned on evacuating—well, until she showed up on his front porch—he hadn't stocked up on much of anything except that water they'd filled in the bathtub. They'd just have to make do with what was there for now and figure out the rest of it later.

She laid blueberry toaster pastries with white frosting and blue sprinkles on one plate and strawberry pastries with a pink glaze and red sprinkles on another. Then she sliced an apple she'd found in a bowl on the counter and divided it evenly between the two plates. The candles on the counter glowed gently, giving the frosting a pearlized glow.

If it hadn't been all so ridiculous, Becca realized she would have found the scene downright domestic—and almost a little romantic.

But she couldn't let herself start thinking that way. Everything Ross had done, he'd done as a friend. A comforting hug. A gentle kiss on the forehead. None of it had anything like *feelings* behind it. That would be crazy. It hadn't even been two days since they'd more-or-less been mortal enemies.

So why could she not put the thoughts of Ross' sheltering arms and the brush of that kiss out of her mind?

Really, the fact that she was still replaying the images in her mind was more ridiculous than the idea of Pop-Tarts by candlelight.

She needed to get control of herself before Ross came back inside. She couldn't let him know what was on her mind. He'd think she was crazy.

All he'd wanted to do was be a supportive friend to her on a crazy, mixed-up day. Instead, she let her mind wander all over the place. Stuff like that used to get her in trouble. She'd come to Port Provident to leave trouble behind.

Which meant she needed to leave thoughts of Ross Reeder behind.

It bothered her to realize she didn't want to.

"Looks like everyone is settled out there." Ross walked in from the back deck, bringing all of her thoughts front and center before they ever had a chance to exit stage right.

"Great." Becca tried to control the slight waver in her voice. She couldn't let Ross know what she'd been thinking. "That should get us through the night, at least."

"It should." His voice seemed far away, even though there wasn't more than a few steps' distance between them.

"I made dinner. Do you prefer blueberry or strawberry?" She held a plate of un-toasted toaster pastries in each hand.

"Blueberry sounds good. Thanks for getting those out."

The sincerity in his voice made her smile. "I hate that the phones are down. When *Le Cordon Bleu* hears about my mad skills in the kitchen, they're going to want to call—and it'll just go straight to voicemail."

Ross threw his head back and laughed. "We *will* probably be cut off from the world for a few days, I'd guess."

"That's okay. I've been on my own before." Becca resisted the urge to lick the Pop-Tart crumbs off her fingers. No matter how much her stomach grumbled, there would not be any seconds tonight.

Ross took his plate of iced pastries to the futon and sat down with an audible sigh of relief, then kicked off his soggy shoes.

"You mean when you left Minnesota?" He asked.

"Wisconsin," Becca corrected. "And yes. But even before that. Bess passed away several months before I left town. And then Rupert passed away a month after she did."

"So, Bess was your grandmother, right? And Rupert was your grandfather?" Ross inhaled the first rectangle of crumbly dough practically in one bite.

Becca crunched on an apple slice. The actions of eating seemed to take some of the tension out of being around Ross for her. She could focus on what was on her plate instead of *those* thoughts.

"No, Rupert was a basset hound. The most loyal companion you could ever have." She hesitated. She rarely talked about Bess and Rupert, and she never spoke about what she was about to say next. But the soft glow of the candlelight gave Becca a sense of protection. She hadn't spoken of Wisconsin in anything more than passing for a decade, but now she felt powerless to stop.

Maybe Hurricane Hope's winds had knocked something loose in her heart.

"I told you about the snake earlier, sort of. Well, not long after that, I was removed from my mother's custody. I only saw her a handful of times during the next thirteen years—not that it was much of a loss. I bounced around foster families for about a year while some legal issues were sorted out, then I went to live with my grandmother, Bess. We'd both been disappointed by my mother, so we always had that in common. We didn't have any money, though. We lived on her pension and Social Security in subsidized housing. But the one thing we did have was Rupert. Rupert knew he was loved—and in return, he gave that back tenfold. He's why I got into working at the animal shelter. Rupert helped me when I needed it most. In his honor, I try to help other animals when they need it most."

Ross sat his plate on the floor. "Wow, I had no idea. But Rupert does sound like a special dog. Reminds me a lot of Cookie. People think that I saved Cookie, but that's not the case. Cookie helped me find my purpose in life."

"Which is?" Becca couldn't even feign containment of her curiosity.

"Supporting our military dogs after they leave the service. Some dogs get adopted by their handlers, but others don't. There have been some even left behind in foreign countries—but thankfully that is happening less often, and some lawmakers are working to change that completely. I believe strongly that we need to take care of all our veterans once their time defending our country is over—and that includes our furriest soldiers, as well. They risk everything with every single job. I treated them daily and held too many paws as they crossed the Rainbow Bridge when there was nothing more I could do."

"The Rainbow Bridge isn't in camo for military dogs?" Becca hated the thought of dogs dying in combat and going to their eternal doggy rest.

"Not that I'm aware of. We want them to find it." Ross gave a half-smile, lost in the memories.

"So, what do you do for the dogs like Cookie?" Becca's curiosity had been piqued.

Ross stood up and brought his paper plate back to the kitchen. "Nothing yet. I'm still working on the plans. I want to facilitate providing forever homes for them. Since it appears to be a total loss across the downstairs of the house where my clinic is—at least as far as

I could tell when I was in there earlier tearing out the kennels and other supplies—that's probably going to set me back a bit."

Becca could definitely identify with that feeling. "So... we're in the same boat."

"I guess we are." Ross folded the plate and stuffed it in the trash can under the sink.

The same need to speak from earlier filled her mind and mouth again. "Ross?"

"Yeah?"

He leaned against the counter casually, and the candlelight fell on half his face, sending the other half into shadow. Becca almost lost her train of thought. She shook her head, trying to get back on track.

"We want the same thing, don't we?" That didn't come out right. She hadn't felt this tongue-tied since she was fifteen, trying to get an invitation to a school dance. Hopefully, Ross would know what she meant.

"What's best for animals who just need love and a good break?"

He *did* understand. Her heart felt lighter. "Yes, exactly."

"Yeah, if that's what you mean, then yes, we do."

She reflected quickly on contentious board meetings, sifting through the memories like the shuffling of a deck of cards. She'd once counted down the minutes in those meetings, just waiting until she could get away from Ross.

Now, she couldn't believe what she was about to say.

"Do you think we could work together on those goals?"

He narrowed his eyes just slightly. Watching their coloring shift in the flicker of the dim light almost made her weak in the knees.

"What are you thinking?"

"Well, I haven't quite put that together yet." She pushed frizz-addled hair back off her forehead and could have kicked herself. Who reaches out for a partner without a plan? Maybe everything Ross said about her was right. She had big ideas with no clue how to accomplish them.

He was right, and her heart began to sink at that realization.

"I've already asked the Beach Patrol team that helped out here tonight to get a message to Rigo Vasquez that we need a more permanent spot for these animals. I'm going to try and get to the city's command center tomorrow and see if there's a space we can use." He put out his right hand. "We'll go together. Care to shake on it, Partner?"

It wasn't quite the same as being wrapped back in his arms, but the grip of his hand was strong as his fingers circled her palm. It would do.

"Becca! Get up—we've got to go." Ross knocked insistently on the bedroom door.

He'd slept on the futon. Becca slept in the main bedroom, and she'd slept like a rock. With no howling winds or driving rain or worries about being swept out to sea and identified only by the Social Security number she'd written on her arm, she hadn't woken once since her head hit the pillow.

Becca didn't especially want to wake up now, but the urgency in Ross' tone of voice told her that sleeping in was not going to be an option.

She rolled off the mattress and shuffled to the door, opening it slowly.

"What's going on?"

"Breakfast," he said with a smile. "And hopefully not Pop-Tarts."

"I don't understand. Your pantry is stocked with them—and not much else."

"Exactly. Someone just came by while I was working on mucking out the clinic. He said First Provident Church is hosting a breakfast this morning for the people who rode out the storm. I don't know what they could possibly be serving, but I don't think it matters much. It's food. Get dressed and let's go before it's all gone."

Becca looked down at her oversized T-shirt and shorts. "Um. I *am* dressed, Ross. What you see is pretty much what you get with me right now. I'll re-do my ponytail. That's probably as fancy as I'm going to get."

He smiled, and Becca felt her cheeks warm slightly. She certainly hadn't packed makeup in her small backpack. The natural look would have to do for right now.

Ross gave her an up-and-down look and then smiled. "I think you're the fanciest woman on Provident Island right now."

"Are you hitting on me, Ross Reeder?" The sass flew out of her mouth before she had a chance to bite her tongue. Too late to take it back now. The best she could hope for was that he thought she was crazy.

"I'm taking you to the best breakfast on the island, aren't I?" His eyes were loaded with mischief.

How could she have never seen this side of him before? She liked this side of Ross—more than she would have ever imagined it was possible to admit.

"You're taking me to the *only* breakfast on the island." She gave him a quick once-over as he walked in front of her to the door of the garage apartment. She liked *this* side of Ross too.

"Oh!" She remembered all the little lives they were responsible for. "Does everyone on the deck have food and water? And Cookie and Polly and the cats too? Let's get them settled before we go."

Ross opened the door, then waited for her on the small landing. "I've been up for three hours, Sleeping Beauty. Everything's taken care of. Don't worry about anything. Let's go see what kind of meal the good people of First Provident can pull together."

Luckily, First Provident was in the middle of the Live Oak Historic District, and Ross' home and clinic were on the very edge of the zone. Walking carefully and dodging debris, the walk took them about thirty minutes, but they were able to fill the time with conversation about animals that had made an impression with them during the years.

Becca felt entirely at ease this morning, which was crazy when she let herself think briefly about how much had changed. She was all but homeless and her place of business—a nonprofit that depended on the generosity of island residents—was a waterlogged mess that might never recover.

But the sun was shining, she was talking about animals she'd loved, and more than that, she was enjoying an easy stroll in the company of the first—and most unexpected—man who'd piqued her interest since she moved to Port Provident.

A large white tent had been erected in the south corner of the First Provident Church parking lot. Rows of tables looked neat and organized. Becca could see fruit and bread and bottles of water stacked along them, as well as some boxes which held other items she wasn't yet close enough to identify.

"I'm so hungry that this looks like a four-star restaurant." The pace of Ross' steps increased once they hit the pavement of the church parking lot.

"Do four-star restaurants have buffets in tents?" Becca wondered aloud. "I've never actually been to one."

"Been to what?"

"A four-star restaurant. My fancy dining experiences are usually casual chains. That's a step up from fast food, which is a step up from microwaveable freezer dinners and ramen noodles."

Ross gave her a sideways glance. "Not even once, like maybe on a vacation or something?"

Becca couldn't stop the laugh that bubbled up. "You're on the board of directors of the Port Provident Animal Shelter. You know what I make a year. Four-star vacations aren't really in the budget. Aren't you the one who is always reminding me I need to stick to the budget?"

"Guilty as charged."

He smiled again, and Becca could feel a five-star level of happiness inside. She'd survived the hurricane. She didn't know what was ahead, but the sun was shining, and she felt a lightness in her spirit that she hadn't felt in a while. She resisted the urge to stomp on the smile resting in her heart—she didn't want to hear that small voice in the back of her mind reminding her that her life had been an exercise in disaster.

Good things just didn't happen to girls from the projects who came from mothers who cared more about drugs than their own children.

Becca knew that voice, knew it too well. It was never far away from her thoughts, and it spoke what she knew was the truth.

She just didn't want to hear it today. "*Sssh...*"

"What?"

Shoot. She'd said that out loud. Ross had heard her.

"Shoo." Becca waved a hand. "I thought there were mosquitoes."

"If there aren't now, there will be soon, I imagine." The line for breakfast was about thirty people deep. Ross and Becca shuffled along. Becca decided to keep the conversation on the important things, like mosquitoes, so she didn't find herself giving her fears a platform to take over her mind.

At the head of the line, Becca saw a familiar face. Diana Peoples, the matriarch of one of the island's oldest families and another board member of the Port Provident Animal Shelter, was handing out bananas to the hungry crowd.

"Oh, my darling Becca, what are you doing here? I thought you were leaving town." Becca gratefully took the curved yellow fruit Diana handed her. "And Dr. Reeder—you too. What are you both doing here, together?"

Diana's look was undeniably skeptical. She'd sat through every single contentious board meeting—and more often than not, played the role of mediator.

"A dog named Polly started it all," Ross answered. "Then some cats in an apartment. And another one on a porch. And then a whole zoo at the shelter over in the high school."

"But we sent all the animals in the shelter up to temporary homes in Houston," Diana said.

Becca grabbed a bottle of water. "Right. These were all animals that got left behind. They needed someone to take care of them, then the causeway closed before we could get back off the island. But what are you doing here, Diana? Surely you have plenty of places you could evacuate to."

Diana leveled her gaze. "Port Provident is my home. This isn't my first hurricane to ride out. It won't be my last, I'm sure. My late father-in-law was a primary force in rebuilding Port Provident in the aftermath of the Great Storm of 1910. I'm needed here. Someone has to organize things like this for our people. The government is never going to take care of Provident Island the way Provident Islanders will. That's just a fact."

Becca couldn't argue with that. They hadn't seen anyone "official" yet during their walk from Ross' house to the church.

"Now give me about five minutes, dear, and then I need to talk to you."

Becca wasn't quite sure what the matriarch could want to talk with her about, but talking with Diana was always enjoyable, no matter the subject. She was unfailingly pleasant—everything Becca had always expected an older, Southern lady to be—and she was knowledgeable about the causes she involved herself with.

"That sounds good, Diana. I'll just go find a place to sit—probably on that curb over there." Becca pointed at a rise of dry concrete to the left. The few chairs that were at the makeshift "four-star restaurant" were all occupied.

Becca and Ross settled themselves and ate dry cereal with raisins out of a miniature box and several pieces of fruit. They enjoyed a companionable silence as they focused on eating. Ross had been right. It was one of the best and most appreciated meals she'd ever tasted.

She tried not to be distracted by thoughts of what—or when— they'd eat next. Without power, water, infrastructure, or a stocked pantry back at the garage apartment, nothing was a given. At least the animals would be able to eat. Ross said that most of his stash of prescription and premium dog food had survived because it was housed in a supply closet on the second floor.

"Dr. Reeder?" A man stood over them.

"Hey, Ben—how can I help you?" Ross stood up, then gestured to Becca. "Becca, this is Detective Ben King with Port Provident PD. Ben, this is Becca Collins, director of the Port Provident Animal Shelter."

"Nice to meet you, Ms. Collins." Ben extended his hand for a brief shake.

"I'm glad I noticed you as I drove by on patrol—or what accounts for patrol right now. What a mess." The detective ran a hand through his hair. "Gizmo and I were out together earlier, and now he's not putting weight on his front right paw. I think he stepped on something. Do you think you could take a look?"

"Sure. Where is he?"

"I dropped him off at the command center at the Grand Provident Hotel. Would you be able to ride over there with me?"

Ross looked at Becca before answering.

"Go ahead," she said. "Diana Peoples said she needed to talk to me, anyway. And it's a pretty straight shot back to the apartment. I'll be fine."

"You sure?" Something about Ross' double-checking made a warmth flow in her veins. It had been a long time since anyone had been truly concerned with Becca's well-being beyond a "how are you?" type of question in passing.

She raised two thumbs. "Positive."

"Ok, I shouldn't be gone too long."

"Do what you need to do. I promise I'll be okay. I'll go back to the apartment and start taking all the animals out for a potty break. I've got plenty to occupy my time."

Becca wasn't alone for long—Diana Peoples joined Becca as she was finishing her bottle of water.

"Have you seen the shelter yet?" Diana asked.

She sat down on the narrow curb, which surprised Becca. Diana always seemed like a very proper lady. She struck Becca as more of the drawing-room-with-silk-curtains type than the sit-on-a-chunk-of-concrete type.

But everything had been turned upside down by Hurricane Hope, and Becca was glad for the older woman's company.

"Unfortunately, yes. We were able to get there yesterday afternoon. I think it will wind up being a total loss."

"And your apartment? Is it destroyed as well?"

For some reason, a lump formed in Becca's throat. She'd never thought of herself as a sentimental person. But admitting to Diana

Peoples that everything was gone made her heart hurt. "Yes, pretty much."

Diana took Becca's hand in her own. Her hand felt cool and soft. It was calming just to know Diana cared. "Did you have insurance?"

"Probably not enough. I know I had the bare minimum on my things in the apartment. And as for the shelter, we had the coverage that was required to be in operation, but not really much more. We just couldn't afford all the bells and whistles."

"I understand." Diana squeezed Becca's hand. "You mentioned taking care of some left-behind animals earlier. Where are they now?"

"Ross' garage apartment. He was able to dismantle some of the kennels in his vet clinic and reassemble them out on his deck so we could keep all the animals safe. But it's not a permanent solution. It's not even a twenty-four-hours-from-now solution. I honestly don't know what we're going to do. Ross was going to try and talk to someone at the city, but...look at everything around us. Some stray dogs are not going to be City Council's priority."

"No, you're probably right." Diana was quiet for a moment, then squeezed Becca's hand again. "But they can be mine."

Becca turned her head and looked Diana straight in the face. Her gray hair had been pulled up into a bun that still managed to look elegant, in spite of the current conditions. "What do you mean?"

"Well, remember I told you back in the line that my father-in-law, John Peoples, helped rebuild this town in 1910?"

Becca nodded.

"Well, our family has continued to play a role in rebuilding after every hurricane since, both with our development company, the Peoples Property Group, and the Peoples Family Foundation, which I run. Hurricane Hope will be no different. And there's no reason that rebuilding work can't start today."

Diana unlaced her hand from Becca's and gave a quick pat on Becca's leg.

"Give me a little bit to get everything lined up—it's a little harder without my cell phone working, but I have a few strings I can pull to get some messages to the right people. Here's what I'm going to do. Peoples Property Group has a property in town that used to be a nursery school. It's sitting vacant right now, and I think the area where it is didn't get as badly hurt as most of the island. I'm going to get my grandson-in-law, the company CFO, to get all the paperwork done. You can move the shelter there, rent-free, for six months. My great-nephew is a contractor based in Austin. He's already scheduled to start working on some projects here next week. I'll just have him come down tomorrow and start working on the school. It won't be anything fancy to begin with, but it'll work."

Becca's jaw dropped. "You'd do all of that for us, just like that?"

"Well of course," Diana said matter-of-factly. "It's all got to be rebuilt sometime. Why not start now? And I wouldn't be doing my duty as an animal shelter board member if I left the animals of this town on Ross Reeder's back porch when I knew there was a better solution."

Her tone was no-nonsense but still gentle. If she'd been in another part of the country, people would have called her a Steel Magnolia. Here, on the Texas Gulf Coast, Becca decided a better description would be Steel Oleander. It suited Diana well.

"Thank you doesn't seem adequate, Diana." While Diana had all the right words at this moment, Becca was at a loss.

"It's my pleasure, Becca. The Bible tells us to love our neighbor— and that of faith, hope, and love, the greatest is love. It says love is patient and love is kind. Well, that's how I feel about Port Provident. I love this island and the people—and the animals—on it."

Becca had heard the Bible quoted more in the last two days than she had in the last ten years. For some reason, though, she was becoming less annoyed with it. Maybe it was because you couldn't really argue with the principle of love.

"Now, about the apartment. Where are you staying, Becca?"

"Well, I spent the hurricane and last night in Ross' garage apartment with him and the zoo."

"When I get direction about the nursery school, I'll have Mitch find you an apartment too. I know there are several in the portfolio available right now." A half-smile pushed across Diana's face. "You know, my dear, there was a time when I'd have said you and Ross were far more likely to survive a hurricane than each other's presence. It looks like you've actually done both."

"A real miracle, eh?" Becca didn't know whether to laugh at the observation or be slightly embarrassed at the way she and Ross had been so adversarial for so long.

"Well, God works in mysterious ways. Did you know that my father-in-law met my mother-in-law when he rescued her out of a tree after the Great Storm? It's a wonderful story. I'll have to tell it to you sometime. But for now, just know that even a hurricane named Hope can be used for hopeful purposes. I think you and Ross could do great things together if you could ever see eye-to-eye."

Great things? Becca thought that might be stretching it, even though her opinion of Ross had done a one-eighty since she showed up on his porch with one of his furry patients.

"I don't know about 'great,' Diana."

"Why not, Becca? You both are far more alike than you realize. And you all are the two most passionate people on this island when it comes to taking care of our animals. I take my own dogs to Ross because he's so devoted. And there's no one who could be more committed to the Port Provident Animal Shelter than you are. I've worked with several directors during my time on the board. You stand out, my dear."

Becca's heart warmed. Bess was the only one who ever complimented her like that. And it had been a long time since Bess…

A tear slipped from her eye. She tried to choke the others back.

"I didn't mean to upset you, Becca." Diana took her hand again, squeezing gently.

"Oh, you didn't." Becca's instinct told her to play it off. But what good would come from being anything but honest with this generous woman? Carefully, she allowed a paper-thin layer over her heart to peel back, like an onion. "You just reminded me of my grandmother who raised me. I knew she loved me."

Diana shifted positions and leaned over, wrapping Becca in a full, warm hug. "Oh, darling Becca. I love you too. It's okay to let your guard down sometimes."

Becca sat, stunned. She didn't know what to say.

All she knew is she'd had two hugs in two days from two different people that had utterly rocked her world.

She'd missed hugs—and she'd never allowed herself to realize it.

If Diana's quote was right and the greatest thing out there was love, the second greatest had to be an unexpected hug.

7

*D*iana Peoples was true to her word. She got messages to all the right people, and by two o'clock the following afternoon, Becca and Ross stood in front of the building which had once housed The Little Lighthouse preschool.

"Becca? Ross?" A dark-haired man in a faded T-shirt, jeans, and work boots kicked a two-by-four out of his way as he walked toward them. "I'm Matt McGregor, Diana's great-nephew."

Matt extended his hand, and Ross shook first, then Becca.

"Thank you for meeting us here so quickly," Becca said.

"I was already planning to be here—my work on the island starts next week, and I'll be here a while—so when Aunt Diana told me you needed some help, all I needed to do was get my pass to get on the island straightened out. You've probably figured out Aunt Diana is the master at getting things like that done."

"She knows everyone," Ross said with a laugh.

Matt unlocked the door to the building. "Indeed. She always has."

Ross smelled a potent combination of heat and damp when the door opened, but it faded more quickly than he'd expected.

"Aunt Diana was right. This place looks like it fared better than probably ninety percent of places on this island. Unbelievable. I see the water line. It's well below the four-foot mark, so we won't have to replace all of the drywall. We can take everything from four feet and below out and then work from there. We'll pull out the carpet in the rooms. Would you be okay with leaving them as concrete, at least for now?"

"Absolutely," Becca said as they walked room-by-room around the building. "The layout here is wonderful. I can see in my head where things can go. And there are enough rooms so that we can keep all the different types of animals separated and happy-with plenty of room left to spare. So much space."

Ross spoke up. "If we can get the rest of the kennels from my clinic dismantled and moved out, we can repurpose them all in here. Same with any we can salvage from the old shelter. They're metal, so we should be able to clean them and re-use. We can open these windows and get some circulation through the building. All we'll need is some elbow grease."

Matt leaned against a desk in the front room. "About three members of my crew will be able to be here tomorrow. So, we've got a few elbows to work with. They're coming from Austin and bringing drywall and whatever else it looks like we'll need after I've done this walkthrough. Let me go take a look at some infrastructure things, and I'll be back shortly."

Ross knew he should be checking out the building and making mental notes. There would be a lot of work to do in a very short period of time to make this all work for the animals in their care. But he couldn't take his eyes off Becca.

She'd piled her long, dark hair on her head in a messy bun today. Women around the world paid stylists hundreds of dollars for hair like Becca's, and yet, she could just effortlessly look like that after two days without a shower. As she walked around the room, her shoulders had lost the slump he'd been so used to seeing.

For years, she'd looked weighed down—to say nothing of how she expressed herself. Where once she'd been touchy, feral...now she seemed in bloom. It was through the drenching flood of the hurricane had finally quenched some kind of thirst inside her.

"Look at this yard, Ross. What a great play area for the dogs. They'll love it. And did you see that sunroom off the back? I can just picture it one day filled with turrets and towers for the cats to climb around on."

He tried to look at the yard, but his gaze wouldn't go past Becca. "I see something else entirely here."

She spun on her heel, face-to-face with him. "What?"

Joy and curiosity filled her face, alight with possibility. Her eyes were almost the color of blackberries, deep and shining with just a hint of cinnamon.

He took a step forward and flicked a wayward strand of hair back from her forehead, then ran his arms from the tops of her shoulders down to just before the elbow. He expected her to pull back.

Actually, he expected himself to pull back.

But he didn't.

When had he ever thrown caution to the wind like this? Never. At least not that he remembered. But a wind as strong as Hurricane Hope's gusts swept through his heart and mind, pushing out the old, rational Ross.

This was a time when there were no Plan Bs. Hurricane Hope had upended everything on the island. Every Port Providenter was starting from scratch.

Even Ross Reeder and Becca Collins.

He leaned down, passing the forehead he'd placed a delicate kiss on the other night. He didn't want a friendly, comforting kiss today. He wanted a tidal wave, a gale-force wind.

He wanted the hurricane.

Everything he'd known, everything he'd ordered to precision in his life-he wanted to blow it away.

He lowered his mouth until it reached Becca's and waited a split second to see what she would do. She tilted her head slightly to the left.

That was all the signal he needed. He raised his arms, wrapping them around her shoulders and pulling his fingers up into the jumbled bun of her hair. There was no mistaking the wave that overtook them both.

At the sound of footsteps in the hall, Ross reluctantly pushed the tide between them back out to sea.

"The air conditioner was up on a platform. I don't even think it got damaged," Matt said. "Once the electricity comes back on, you should be able to cool down in here without any problems."

Ross didn't want to correct Matt, but judging by the way he could still feel his pulse pounding in his veins, he didn't think there were any chances of cooling off in the near future.

~

Whoa. She'd just kissed Ross Reeder.

The last time she'd seen her mother, Darla Collins had tried to impart dating advice to her only daughter. But she'd put away about four gin and tonics before sharing the life lessons, and so the whole conversation was a miserable, judgmental, harsh failure.

But yet, Becca still remembered every single word.

"Don't you give in," her mother had slurred. "Or they'll take everything they can get."

Becca pushed a deep breath out her nose as she painfully bit her lip. She'd definitely given in.

"Becca?" Ross asked. Matt had left for the mainland so he could call his crew and fill them in on what they need to bring. She and Ross were alone again.

Becca crossed her arms over her chest and slowly looked at Ross.

The expression on his face could only be described as sheepish. "I guess I owe you an apology," he said.

Oh, no...that wasn't in the Darla Collins Dating Manual. There was no troubleshooting part of the book for men who accepted responsibility. And there was definitely not a section on apologies.

Especially unnecessary ones. This one was not on Ross. It was all on her.

But how could she tell him that? She'd already revealed enough about her messed up childhood to him.

"No, really, you don't owe me an apology." It was the truth. Maybe if she didn't say any more, they could just leave it at that.

A shadow crossed his face, and she could see steel settle in his brow. "If I don't owe you an apology, then that means you were okay with it. And if you were okay with it, you wouldn't be acting like you are right now. Thirty minutes ago, you were on cloud nine, twirling around this place like a ballerina. Now you're stomping around angry, like you're in an MMA cage fight. It's either one or the other, Becca. I don't want to apologize—I liked what happened—but I will if I read you wrong. We've come too far to go back to our old corners, our old ways of being offended with one another."

As usual, he was thoughtful and correct. They had come too far. She didn't want to go backward.

A ray of sunshine fell through the window, cutting through the overcast haze that had popped in and out of the sky this afternoon.

She needed to let the light into this conversation. "You don't owe me an apology. You didn't read me wrong."

His brow softened slightly. "So… if I didn't read you wrong, what's happened?"

"It's just…" She bit her lip again. There was no way to say this without sounding ridiculous.

"Just?" He prompted her when the silence stretched on too long.

"Something my mother said a long time ago." She spat the words out like a mouthful of stale cereal.

Ross paused a moment. The look on his face was very thoughtful and compassionate.

"Becca," he said deliberately and reached out his hand. "I don't even know what your mother said, but I can tell it wasn't good."

"No," she replied flatly.

"Give me your hand," Ross said, wiggling the fingers on his outstretched hand.

Tentatively, Becca did as she was asked. It felt silly to hesitate about holding his hand after a kiss like they'd just shared. But she did —further proof that she was just messed up all the way around.

He held her hand for a moment before speaking. The temperature equalized between their fingers. She noticed the palm of her hand warming.

"It seems like you had a pretty crummy childhood where your mother was concerned."

She nodded in agreement. She couldn't bring herself to confirm his observation with words. He'd thrown the dart and hit the target right on the bulls-eye.

"Is there anything she's said to you or done for you that you put particular stock in?"

Becca could feel the steady beat of Ross' pulse in the strong rise below the base of his thumb. She thought about his question for a moment, sorting through memories in her mind.

"No, not really." She spoke quietly and shrugged.

He began to brush the pad of his thumb just below the base of the knuckles on the back of her hand. The touch felt gentle, like velvet.

"Then why are you letting whatever she said have a bearing on you now? You don't need to. She's not here. She'll never be here. You're a strong, independent woman. You dared to get on a bus and create a new life for yourself. You run a successful non-profit organization. You even made it through a hurricane."

Something about Ross' words broke through the fragile glass that had surrounded her heart for years. Why was she letting her mother in this moment? If Darla Collins knocked on her front door tomorrow, Becca knew she probably wouldn't open it.

So why was Darla living rent-free in her head?

That stopped now. It was time for an eviction.

Becca moved her hand and raised it to Ross' cheek, then placed the other hand on his other cheek and leaned in as she took a purposeful step forward. She pulled his head down toward hers and closed her eyes.

Another set of words from a much wiser lady popped into her mind. And this time, she let them stay there.

"*The greatest of these is love,*" Diana Peoples had quoted yesterday.

Becca didn't know if she was falling in love with Ross Reeder, or what, exactly. But she knew if she lived in the past, hearing the voices and the ghosts of a time she'd rather forget, then she'd never know what love was when the time was right to let it in her life.

Ross pulled her closer and as they both gave in to the kiss and the emotion that filled the space between them, time was no longer rewinding. It was standing still.

～

She'd never thought much about the Bible—and certainly never considered it a dating guide—but maybe there was something to those worn-out and often-quoted verses after all.

One sweat-drenched week later, there wasn't a swipe of grease left in either of Ross' elbows. But he did have pride to spare. They'd done it. Animals would be moving in by dinner time. The power and water had recently been restored to Port Provident. They wouldn't be relying on generators or the partnership for bottled water that they'd established with one of the agencies who brought meals to Port Provident's neighborhoods three times a day via a mobile food truck.

"What do you think?" Ross didn't really need to ask Becca the question, he could see the answer written all over her face.

"I. Love. It." Her words were deliberate for maximum emphasis. "This place is more than I could ever have imagined. It makes the plans I had for that old police substation seem so small."

"It definitely reminds me of something straight out of the book of Ephesians."

Becca uncapped a bottle of water and took a drink. "What do you mean?"

Ross stared at the bottle of water, wondering if they had any more behind the front counter. "It's a book in the Bible. In Ephesians 3, it says God is able to do more than we can ask or imagine—or at least that's my paraphrase of it."

She boosted herself up on the top of the high counter, water bottle still in hand. "I like that. Tell me more."

Her request was not what Ross expected to hear. He remembered back to the night of Hurricane Hope, when she'd told him and his Bible verses what she'd thought of them and where they could go. He was glad that he was on the opposite side of the counter, rummaging for a water of his own, so that Becca couldn't see the look of surprise on his face.

"The next verse goes on to give God the glory for His works. We should too. This place is definitely a miracle on many levels."

"Agreed. But...like what do you do? Is there like one of those chants or creeds or something you're supposed to say?"

Ross popped himself up on the counter next to her. "Well, maybe. But tell me, what do you like better? A formal note printed on letterhead with some prewritten words of thanks typed in the middle with a signature scrawled at the bottom or a short but sincere 'thank you' straight from the person you've helped?"

"The right answer is number two, isn't it?" She screwed the cap back on the now-empty bottle and sent it flying in the air toward the trash can. It made a loud thunk as it rattled straight through the top opening.

"I don't think there is a right answer, Becca. When it comes to matters of the heart, there rarely is a protocol. What matters is the right motivation, I've always thought."

"So, it doesn't matter if I really don't know how to pray or any of that?"

"Nope." He put his water bottle down and took her hands in one of his own. "What matters is what's right here."

Ross pointed his finger at her chest, then traced a heart, hovering just barely over the cotton of her V-neck T-shirt. Then he let his finger brush the bottom of her collarbone.

Becca shuddered slightly, and the lightning ran back through Ross, too.

He'd never felt this way about another woman in so short a time.

This had become so real, so fast. He wanted to be around Becca, talk to her, find out more about her, hold her.

"Can you help me?" She breathed out the words. "I want to say thank you."

Ross took her hands and clutched them between his own, folding them into the traditional position for prayer.

"Thank you, God, for knowing that we'd be here and already putting in place the plans for the Port Provident Animal Shelter to be better than ever, even after something as destructive as a hurricane. Thank you for taking our dreams beyond what we could ask for or imagine. Thank you for seeing our heart and knowing just what we need and what we can't always express adequately."

Ross paused. Becca punctuated his prayer with a simple "Amen."

She kept her head bowed slightly. The loose hair that had come out of her ponytail fell in a messy cascade down the side of her face.

"I don't think I've ever prayed like that before. I've never had anything more to say than 'now I lay me down to sleep'—and even then, I stopped saying that by junior high when Bess no longer tucked me in at night. She was the only reason I ever said it."

"Well, maybe now you have some reasons of your own."

She looked up, the hair falling clear of her face. Ross could see a light in the corner of Becca's eye.

"I think maybe I do."

The sound of heavy-soled footwear announced Matt McGregor before he ever set foot in the front intake room.

"Can you believe it? We did it. I'd love to have you both on a work crew sometime. You were non-stop."

Ross was intrigued by the idea. There was going to be a lot of work to do to bring Port Provident back to what it had been only a week or so before. He liked the idea of rolling up his sleeves and pitching in for the good of the community. He'd come to Port Provident after a lifetime of moving here and there with the military—both as a kid and an adult—and he wanted to get to a place where he put down roots.

"You know, we've worked alongside each other for the better part of a week, but I don't know exactly what you do, Matt. I guess we were just too busy for chit-chat. I know your great-aunt said you were a contractor."

Matt laughed a little. "Well, not exactly. Aunt Diana is close. I started working with Peoples Property Group here, heading up the remodeling projects. Then—you guessed it—I met a girl. I followed her to Austin and hung out my own shingle, so to speak, building custom homes. When the housing market went soft about two years ago, a friend asked me to come work with him at Helping Hands Homes—the group that goes around rebuilding homes for people who can't afford housing themselves. I now head up operations for our entire Southern region, which includes Texas. So, that's really why my crew and I are here. We're going to start Monday rebuilding homes through Helping Hands."

"Oh wow. I volunteered on a Helping Hands site in Houston about three years ago," Becca said. "It was incredible to be a part of something that so drastically changed lives. I guess it's kind of like what I do at the shelter. I change the lives of the animals—and the people who adopt them into forever homes. I love being a part of something bigger than me."

"That's exactly it, Becca. I've always been very satisfied with the work I do, the jobs I've held. I love building. I always have. But the two years I've spent with Helping Hands have been really rewarding." He stepped behind the counter and knelt down, in search of one of the last bottles of water. "We've got a big job ahead of us here in Port Provident. Being in a non-profit, you'll understand when I say this—I know we can do the work. I just hope we can raise all the funds necessary to do what we're capable of."

"I completely understand that." Becca nodded emphatically. "Every dollar counts."

"And hopefully, once Port Provident gets back on its feet, you'll be able to use this new building to grow your mission too," Matt said.

"Well, we're only here temporarily. But I'd love to find a way to stay here permanently." She elbowed Ross playfully. "This is the money guy on our board of directors. He told me I couldn't afford the last building I wanted to move to. We'll see if he finds a way to let me stay here."

Ross raised an eyebrow. He didn't want to be the bad guy, standing between animals and good care and forever homes. But he couldn't help it—Becca was right. He was the planner, the analyzer.

"Well, things can work out to be more than we ask or imagine, Becca." He raised the other eyebrow as he re-surfaced their earlier conversation.

Matt polished off his water with one long gulp. "Oh, Ephesians. I love that verse."

The next morning, Becca was stocking dog food in the supply room when Ross stuck his head around the corner of the door frame.

"These were just delivered for you." He raised his hand. A key ring with two silver-colored keys was pinched between his thumb and forefinger. "Want to go check it out?"

It wasn't exactly ringing a bell. "What's that to?"

"Becca." Ross' voice couldn't hide the disbelief. "Your new apartment. Remember your fairy godmother, Diana Peoples?"

"Ha. How could I forget her? I just didn't know when the apartment was coming. My contact at Peoples Property Group didn't give me a date. We were just focused on doing what we needed to, so we could get the shelter up and running first."

"Well, all the animals are moved in. Now it's your turn." Ross jingled the keys again. "Cookie's a great roommate, but he's more of the silent type. It was nice to hear another voice around the house. But I will definitely not miss sleeping on the futon."

"I still feel bad about that. You should have put me out there. You didn't need to give up the real mattress and box spring."

Ross grabbed the last two oversized bags of kibble and wedged them on the top shelf. "What? And leave you in the living room with two snoring dogs and the pickiest passel of cats this side of the Mississippi? You'd have never gotten any beauty sleep."

"Beauty sleep? Have you seen me lately? Ponytails, no makeup, and the same stained shirt four days in a row." Becca flicked at her ponytail. "You're either lying or chivalry isn't dead, but it certainly is blind. And maybe lacking an ability to smell."

Ross wrapped his arms around her waist and turned her to face him. "I'm not blind, and I'm not lying."

He grinned and the smile that showed his white teeth belonged to a pirate far more than a knight of some round table. He leaned down and kissed her tenderly, pushing all thoughts of ponytails and sweat-stained shirts aside.

"But," he said as he slowly pulled back. "My nose is in perfect working order, and I hope his new place of yours has a nice, hot shower."

Becca gave him a playful slap on the cheek. "Dead. Chivalry is so dead."

"Take these." Ross placed the keys in her hand, then folded her fingers down over the palm to secure them. "At least I know you won't hit me again if you have house keys to hold on to. Let's go see your new place."

The apartment was just off one of the best-known downtown streets. She hadn't initially recognized the address, but once Becca saw the building, her heart fluttered a bit. The Hinckman-Mercer building was one of the best-known buildings in Port Provident. It was a stunning example of Victorian architecture that had earned a spot on the National Register of Historic Places—as well as every other similar designation. A few years ago, Port Provident had buzzed with details of the painstakingly accurate—and very costly—complete renovation of all six floors of the building. The bottom floor was retail. Floors two and three were small offices. And floors four through six were designated as residential.

Becca looked down at the key ring. The number taped to the flat top of one of the keys read "600."

The penthouse suite? Surely, it couldn't be.

Regardless of the floor, it would be a bit more challenging to get from downtown to her place of work than it had been in her previous commute down the main hall at the old Port Provident Animal Shelter. But she'd figure out a way to make it work and make sure the animals were cared for during the overnight hours.

When there was a will, there was a way.

Or, as Ross put it—there were solutions waiting that we couldn't even imagine to our problems.

And she was about to walk through the door of one of those above-and-beyond blessings. Diana Peoples' generosity blew her away just as though she was one of so many palm fronds during Hurricane Hope. Diana not only had the ideas, she had the means to pull them off. She just plain made things happen.

Becca hesitated slightly at the door, then put the key in the lock and turned.

As she opened the door, the first thing she noticed was the light streaming in through the panes of thick, historic glass. An old Beatles song about the sun popped into her head, and she started humming.

"Yeah, this *is* alright." Ross picked up on the tune and joined in. "Doo doo-de-doo de-doo-doo-doo."

She couldn't believe what she was seeing. The room was straight out of a fancy architectural or design magazine. "It's even furnished, Ross."

He picked up a hand-written note from the table by the door and began to read.

"Dear Becca, I hope this apartment will meet your needs. It has been used by Provident Medical School as a corporate-style apartment for visiting professors and the like, but with classes and operations canceled indefinitely at the medical school, there won't be anyone using it for several months at the least. I am pleased to tell you that you may stay here, rent-free until Provident Medical resumes operations and needs this back. Thank you for all you do for the animals of Port Provident. You are truly a blessing to the furry "least of these" on our fair island. With gratitude and sincere best wishes for your new home, Diana Powell Peoples. PS—Tell Polly 'Welcome Home' for me as well. I hope she enjoys her time here."

Becca's legs wobbled beneath her, and she reached for a chair to steady herself.

"Unbelievable," she said quietly.

Ross placed the letter back on the side table and began exploring around. "You can see the harbor from here—all the way down to where it meets the Gulf of Mexico. What an incredible view."

The inside of the penthouse was just as incredible. "Look at all the detail, Ross. The thick plaster on the walls, that amazing medallion on the ceiling that holds the light—can you believe that scroll design? These floors!"

Becca's eyes darted from one historically-accurate detail to another. "Come look at the bedroom, Ross! They've done the walls with shiplap in here!"

She ran into the bathroom on feet that barely touched the ground. "Oh, and a claw foot bathtub. I haven't had a bathtub in years, just a shower. I want a bubble bath so badly right now, I'm about to start drooling."

Ross gave her one of his trademark cocky looks. "Oh, drool will go great with all the sweat in that shirt, Beck."

She raised her hand in a mock threat. Ross ducked.

"Hey now. Can we just hug instead?"

A military man who practiced hug diplomacy. Ross Reeder was nowhere near the man she'd once thought he was. She walked over to his outstretched arms.

He was more than she could ever have asked for or imagined.

8

*B*ecca dropped the last scoop of kibble in the bowl near two Pomeranians. There were rumors that the main grocery store in the center of the island would be re-opening soon, but it would probably still be a few more days until conveniences like that were once again a part of Port Provident life. The residents of the new Port Provident Animal Shelter had now finished every bag and can of cat and dog food that had been able to be saved from Ross' veterinary clinic and from the old shelter building.

So, Ross had volunteered to take Becca's car and drive to the mainland and bring back enough food for at least another week.

As the sun began to streak the sky with glowing shades of red and gold behind gentle wisps of cloud, Becca began to get nervous. He'd been gone most of the day for what should have been a three-or-four-hour trip at the maximum. Had this been the day when her car finally decided to give up?

She began sweeping the concrete floors as a means of getting her mind on other things. Just as she was finishing the back room where the larger dogs stayed, Becca heard the lock turn in the back door.

"I'd give just about anything for a wheelbarrow or a cart or something right now. Thirty-pound bags of dog food are heavy. Twenty thirty-pound bags of dog food could be considered the equivalent of a CrossFit workout," Ross squeezed through the door with a bag covering most of his upper body.

Becca held open the door, then ran ahead, opening the door to their supply room and trying to make sure Ross had clear passage.

"Let me help you with that," she said.

"These are way too heavy. It reminds me of running with all my gear in the Army." Ross rolled the bag off his shoulders onto the floor, then kicked it with the toe of his shoe to where he wanted it. "There are a bunch of smaller bags of cat food and flats of canned food. You get those. I'll get the dog food and the bags of cat litter."

It took about thirty minutes to get everything unloaded and organized, but when they finished, it brought a smile to Becca's face to see their supply room becoming stocked. In her mind, she kept a running list of all the other things they needed. But for right now, the animals in her care had food, water, shelter, and love.

What more could anyone ask for?

Becca looked at Ross, and the same thoughts ran through her head. She had been given the use of a phenomenal apartment and space in which to conduct her life's work. Plus, she was coming to care more about Ross with every hour she spent in his presence—actually, that wasn't completely accurate.

She was coming to care more about Ross every hour, period, whether he was around or not. The fact that he hadn't left her thoughts all afternoon, even though he'd driven into Houston to pick up supplies for the shelter proved that. Becca didn't know how the other side of a hurricane could bring about the happiest times she'd felt in years, but it had.

Becca's stomach rumbled, and she remembered that of her "food, water, shelter and love" list, the one thing she was missing was food.

"Ross, do you know what time it is?"

He wiped a trail of sweat from his forehead, then looked at his watch. "About five-forty-five. Why?"

"Just want to make sure I don't miss the Samaritan's Cross truck. My tummy is grumbling at me." She picked up a few cans of cat food and stacked them on a low shelf. "They usually come around six. I don't have much of anything to eat in the apartment. I can't wait for the grocery store to open back up. I'll be eating this Fancy Feline tuna delight if I don't keep my ears open."

"No, you won't." Ross put his hand on the small of her back and ushered her out of the supply room and over to the chair behind the front desk. "Sit right here and give me a few minutes."

Becca did as she was told, but after so many days of running on adrenaline and working from sun up to sun down at the shelter, Becca struggled with merely sitting still. She couldn't settle down—she felt guilty about not doing something.

"What are you talking about?"

Ross held up a palm. He looked like a crossing guard in a school zone, trying to stop traffic. "Just sit. I'll be right back."

"Ooookay." Becca wasn't convinced. But she didn't see a good alternative, so she complied with Ross' request.

The sound of bells soon alerted Becca to the coming presence of the Samaritan's Cross mobile food truck. Every day, the trucks wound through the neighborhoods of Port Provident, serving up meals—some quite surprisingly tasty, and others downright questionable—to the hungry citizens who had run out of stockpiled meal supplies of their own.

"Ross!" Becca yelled. "The truck is coming. Can I please get out of the chair?"

She held back a laugh at herself. Never in her life did she remember asking a man for permission for doing something she wanted to do. She had always possessed a take-charge personality, a person who acted first and asked questions—or forgiveness—later. What was happening to her?

"No. I'm almost done." Ross' voice was kind but clear. "Give me one more minute."

"But I'm going to miss the truck!"

He reappeared in the doorway, shirt streaked with fading sweat and his hair sticking in ten different directions. Becca forgot that she was agitated about the food truck that would soon appear. The sight of

Ross, looking chiseled under his worn-out shirt stopped every other thought in her head.

"We don't need the truck tonight." He gestured out the back door. "Dinner is served."

What breath there was left in Becca's body vanished as she stepped through the door to the back patio.

Small white tea lights were lined up with precision around the perimeter of the concrete, their petite orange flames flickering with the night's gulf breeze. A white tablecloth had been stretched over the old picnic table the nursery school had left behind. In the center was a jar half-filled with sand, then topped with shells. More tea lights formed concentric circles around it, and the glass of the jar reflected the glow of the candles back into the night.

Becca saw white china and heavy silver utensils arranged with precision. Even the glasses appeared to be crystal, with intricate cutwork around the bottom of the goblet.

She wasn't sure if she would ever be able to pick her jaw up from the ground. This was unbelievable. It was gorgeous. And Ross had clearly put it all together just for her.

But how?

"I hope it's okay that we have some company." Ross gestured toward two furry shadows sitting at attention out in the grass.

Cookie held his fuzzy chartreuse tennis ball between his front-most teeth. It stuck out beyond his nose like a half-eaten snow cone. But just a little further down, Becca could see something else on Cookie.

"Is that a bow tie?"

Ross whistled and lifted a flat hand, palm down. At the sound, Cookie also raised his paw. If a dog could look genteel, sweet cream-colored Cookie fit the description perfectly.

"It's a four-star restaurant. There's a dress code." Ross said, as if that adequately explained why a Labrador retriever was wearing part of a tuxedo.

Polly sat next to Cookie. She had pink bows around the top of each floppy ear and a string of oversized costume pearls wrapped around her neck.

"I feel under-dressed now." Becca looked at her cutoffs and T-shirt from a long-ago fun run. "No one's ever accused me of being a clothes horse, but I've just been out-dressed by two dogs."

Ross shook his head. "Don't worry about it. They've been planning this all day. You were surprised by it—no time to plan."

Becca narrowed her eyes to a squint and cocked her head. "*They've* been planning this all day?"

"Well, I was responsible for the execution. But when I told them this morning, they both wagged their tails."

Becca laughed. "Seal of approval."

"Exactly," Ross said and gestured toward the bench at the back of the picnic table. "I hope everything has earned one from you as well."

"It's wonderful, Ross, but I don't understand." Becca sat down and placed the cloth napkin in her lap. "Where did you find crystal and linen in Port Provident?"

Ross sat on the bench across from her. "I didn't. A long-time friend of mine owns Lavendou 713 in Houston. It's a French bistro. I made a phone call and picked it all up while I was in town today."

"A French bistro?"

"Michelin-rated. Four stars. You said you'd never been to a four-star restaurant before."

A lump rose in Becca's throat. He'd heard what she'd said. And even in the aftermath of a natural disaster, he'd wanted to make something special happen.

Just for her.

With the exception of good-hearted Bess, Becca had spent most of her life around people who only considered themselves.

In fact, if she was honest, Becca had become one of those people. She'd isolated herself with the animals here in Port Provident and rarely took advice from anyone—as evidenced by every board meeting she'd ever sat in with Ross Reeder.

But Ross was different. And he made her want to be different, too.

Becca sat quietly as he placed an expertly-seared steak with mushroom sauce and garlic mashed potatoes and braised vegetables on her plate. Then he leaned down and crisscrossed two stalks of herbs atop the scoop of potatoes. Their tiny purple flowers and slim green leaves provided the perfect accent to the elegant meal.

"What's that?"

"Rosemary," Ross said, as he took his meal out of the white to-go containers and arranged it on his plate in the same style as he'd done on Becca's. "Legend says Venus, the Roman goddess of love, wore rosemary when she rose out of the sea when she was born. Shakespeare wrote about it in Hamlet, saying 'there's rosemary, that's for remembrance.' I want you to remember tonight. Against all odds, I find myself falling for you, Becca Collins—and I don't want you to forget that or explain it away."

"I wish I knew some fancy lines from Shakespeare or words in French. Maybe then I'd know what to say back." She reached a hand across the table, feeling the cool of the cloth on the back side of her hand and the warmth of Ross' palm as he laid it on hers. "But for now, English will have to do. I feel the same way, Ross. I can't believe it took a hurricane to make me see the person you truly are. I want to make it up to you for all the years I misjudged you and was so difficult toward you."

The tea lights made a pattern of dazzle and glow on their hands. Becca knew if she looked inside her heart, she'd see the same sparkling illumination throughout.

"I don't want to worry about the past, Becca. The past doesn't define me, and it isn't going to define you any longer. It's not going to define *us*. Let's just agree that from right now, this moment, we move forward. And we do that with honesty and respect and love."

He said love. She knew he didn't mean it as "in love" but that didn't matter. No one had ever directed that word at her, ever—except Bess, and a grandmother's protective love was something different entirely.

Becca couldn't keep the verse Diana had shared out of her mind. *The greatest of these is love.*

Now she understood why. It had the power to push away the past and lay down a path for the future.

"Honesty, respect, love. I like the sound of that…actually, I *love* the sound of that."

Faith, hope, love and a four-star meal. Never had her life seemed so magical or complete.

Ross carried a file folder of documents into the trailer that served as Billy Patterson's temporary insurance office. He wasn't exactly sure what he'd need, so he'd brought everything he could find.

He knocked at the door and Billy opened it quickly.

"Hey, Ross—thanks for coming over today. I stopped back by the vet clinic late yesterday afternoon to check on a few loose ends, but I didn't see you." Billy slid into the back of the booth in the trailer's dining room area, which now appeared to serve as his desk and client meeting area.

"I had to go to Houston and run some errands. I'm helping Becca Collins get the animal shelter back up and running, and we were out of dog food."

"You know, some lady was up here yesterday asking about her and the shelter. I told her I didn't really know much. I think Larson's agency handles her insurance. She's not a client of mine."

Ross smiled. "We'll work on that…well, depending on how you get my claim settled."

They shared a collective laugh. Billy also had a military background and he and Ross had become friends not long after Ross moved to Port Provident.

"Well, I don't know if you'll like the news I've got for you or not, but the bottom line is this: I think your clinic is a total loss. The upstairs of the house, as you know, is fine except for the roof. That will need to be completely redone. But all your equipment was downstairs. It's gone. There's not anything I would even try and salvage on the bottom floor of your clinic. Your X-ray and some other equipment was leased, so we'll have to settle all of that separately."

Ross drummed his fingers on the manila folder in front of him. "So, what's that mean, Billy?"

"It means that, at a minimum, you're out of that clinic for six months. Maybe longer. You're looking at a total rebuild."

Ross' heart sank. Thankfully, the Army had paid for his schooling, so he didn't have student loans or anything like that hanging over his head. But he still needed to eat and had other bills to pay, and being relatively new in practice here, he didn't have a lot of savings to stretch. Six months—or more—would be a long time to go without a paycheck. It was one of the hazards of being self-employed. He had to admit he'd never fully thought through what opening a practice on an island might mean in the case of a hurricane. He tried to reassure himself that no one could have truly prepared themselves for something like this, unless they'd seen it before.

But still, he realized he hadn't put together a Plan B years ago when he had the opportunity, and he wanted to kick himself over it now.

His insurance agent continued to deliver bad news. "Your truck's a total loss too, but I think that's no surprise to you."

"Yeah, I told her goodbye the night of the storm. It was clear the ol' girl wasn't going to make it."

Billy flipped through a few papers. "You should be able to get a settlement on the truck quickly, so hopefully we can get you some new wheels soon. It's not going to be a settlement that will buy you a brand-new truck with all the bells and whistles, though. That's just how depreciation goes. But I will try and get that expedited for you with the carrier. How about I call you in two or three days with an update on that?"

"Sounds good."

Billy pulled out a few sheets of paper with tiny type on it and laid them in front of Ross. "So, we should go over this quickly."

Ross scanned the paperwork as best he could, but it didn't mean a whole lot to him. "Ok, what is it?"

"It's your business interruption insurance. I've put in a claim for you already, so that's already in process. I'll let you know when it's approved. That will pay your expenses until you're able to open up again. I'll just need some details from you on your budget and average daily income. Here are some notes on what I'll need you to bring me by the end of the week as supporting documentation for your claim."

Billy handed a piece of paper with a list of bulleted items to Ross, who tucked it into his folder with his other necessary paperwork.

"So, what you're saying is I shouldn't worry about paying the bills while we're closed because this will take care of that for me."

"That's what it's designed to do. That's why I make sure all my business-owner clients down here have this as a part of their policy package."

At least someone had thought of a Plan B. That's why it was good to surround yourself with quality people. Everyone could do their part. He'd seen a lot of that since Hope came to town—Becca risking her own chance to evacuate so she could help a dog in need, Rigo Vasquez going from house-to-house in deep water to check on citizens, Diana Peoples putting the resources of one of the island's oldest businesses behind helping to get the Port Provident Animal Shelter back up and running.

He took a deep breath. Things looked a little bleak right now with an anticipated six months of closure for the clinic and no truck. But he knew Billy would do his best to take care of the claims. He'd have a new vehicle of some kind, and this business interruption insurance sounded like it would take care of the day-to-day things until the doors to his little clinic in the Victorian house could re-open.

"Thanks for looking out for me, Billy. Everyone needs a good friend who knows how to navigate all this." Ross pushed out from the booth and stood up.

Billy gave a firm handshake as they walked to the door. "My pleasure, Ross. I love Port Provident and want the best for the town and the people who live here. I'm not the mayor or anything, but I am a man with a plan for helping to bring us back, at least in my own way."

∼

Ross swung open the trailer door. "It's definitely going to take all of us working together. Glad you're in my corner."

Ross brought Becca's car back to the shelter with just enough time to get her to her new apartment and then get back to his own garage apartment before the dusk-to-dawn curfew kicked in. They'd be cutting it close, but if Becca was ready to go, they could probably still make it to their respective homes in time.

When he walked in the door, he found Becca sitting in the middle of the room where the large dogs were housed.

"Beck, we've got to go, or we're going to get caught out after curfew."

"It's Polly, Ross. She's not acting quite right. I'm not leaving here tonight. You head on home. I'll see you in the morning, okay?"

Ross sat down next to Polly and began stroking her head. She looked up at him with soft brown eyes, and Becca's heart melted like snow in Texas over the display of tenderness given and returned.

"What's wrong, girl?"

He began doing a cursory check up and down Polly's furry body.

"She's stayed on her prescription food, right?" He held up Polly's top lip, and ran a finger over her gums, checking her teeth.

"Yes, the whole time. But I think she hasn't gotten enough water. Everything has been so hectic. And it's so hard to keep a kidney patient hydrated, even in the best of times."

Ross felt for a pulse, then pinched the skin near Polly's hind leg three times in a row. "You're spot-on. All signs point to dehydration right now. There could be something more, but I don't have the equipment to check here. I did bring over some electrolyte solution and some IV equipment from my supply room to the one here. If you'll get Polly comfortable on one of the beds, I'll go get what we need. Cookie and I will stay here tonight with you both, just in case."

"You don't have to do that."

"I do. Polly's my patient. If she gets worse, I'll break curfew and drive her to the emergency vet clinic on the mainland." Ross gave Polly one more scratch under the chin and then stood up and headed in search of what he needed.

Becca searched around and found some bedding large enough to accommodate Polly and coaxed her to curl up and get comfortable. Ross came down and quickly hooked up the IV for her and rigged the bag to hang off a shelf.

He sat down beside her and stroked her head until she fell asleep. Cookie lumbered over and laid down, his nose facing Polly's. As he adjusted his position, he dropped his tennis ball from his mouth and pushed it toward Polly's snout with a gentle nudge.

Becca's heart swelled at the trusting gesture of friendship. Quietly, she walked around to Ross' side and sat down. He pulled his free arm around her waist and drew her in, tucking her body up close to his. She let out a breath and felt her shoulders fall. She hadn't realized how much tension she'd been carrying.

"She's going to be okay, Becca. I'll make sure of it."

Becca nodded. "I don't usually get attached to the dogs in my care like this. But Polly and I—we've been through a lot in a short period of time. Sometimes, I have to remind myself that she's not actually my dog."

Polly's breathing shifted to a hearty snore. Ross removed his hand from the dog's back and wrapped it around Becca. His arms completely encircled her body.

Becca believed Ross' words. She believed he would protect Polly, take care of the sweet Labrador. More than that, Becca believed that Ross would take care of *her*, as well.

After a few minutes, Ross spoke. "I got a phone call this afternoon."

"Oh? Your insurance agent?"

"Actually, no. The lady in San Antonio who helped me get reunited with Cookie after he came back from Iraq."

"There really is such a thing? I figured you just picked Cookie up from the Army." Becca leaned her head on Ross' shoulder.

"Well, dogs that are designated as Military Working Dogs—MWDs —they are adopted out of Lackland Air Force Base in San Antonio. But Cookie was technically what's known as a Contract Working Dog —a CWD. Those adoptions are handled privately."

"There are different types of dogs working in combat zones?" Becca hadn't even imagined that there would be such a thing. "I figured a military dog was a military dog."

"Nope. MWDs are trained by the military—the 341st Training Squadron at Lackland is the DoD's Military Working Dog school. When those dogs retire, the DoD handles their retirement and placement. But there are other dogs who work with our soldiers who are trained with private companies. When they retire, they are processed by the companies they work for. That could mean they get left overseas, or that they're brought back to the States and then they go through a private adoption process. It's similar to what you do with the dogs you work with. In Cookie's case, I tracked Cookie down before he even retired and had someone following his movements for me so that I could adopt him—I didn't have official priority since I wasn't Cookie's handler, but luckily, they recognized that Cookie and I had a bond based on my treatment of him."

"So, what was the phone call about?" Curiosity definitely had the best of Becca now.

"Gina's just got a few dogs that need some vet care, and she was wondering if I could come to the ranch in San Antonio and spend a few days helping her out with that. Her long-time vet recently retired."

"So, when are you going?" For reasons she couldn't explain, Becca felt a little nervous at the thought of Ross being gone. "*Pfft.*" Becca let out a half snort as she thought about it.

She tried to push away the shreds of trepidation. Just because she liked having Ross in her life did not mean she needed to turn into one of those clingy women from chick-flick TV movies.

"What?"

"Nothing. Sorry. When are you going?" The only thing worse than thinking crazy thoughts was letting Ross know she was thinking crazy thoughts. She needed to make sure her mouth stayed shut when her mind was running to wherever it was going.

"Probably in the next day or two, if you're okay with that."

Do. Not. Let. Him. Know. Becca. "Oh, sure…why wouldn't I be?"

"No reason. You're more than capable of handling everything

here." He kissed the crown of her head, right where she'd parted her hair. All her doubts faded and the rushing thoughts in her mind slowed to a halt.

They'd worked out a good partnership here at the new shelter, but he was right. She could absolutely handle things for a few days. "Absolutely. Most of the residents of Port Provident—both two-legged and four-legged—are still gone. I've got a good routine going with the animals who are staying here. My biggest problem while you're gone will be deciding what to put in my cart when the grocery store opens back up."

Ross threw his head back and laughed. Polly stirred a bit at the noise, but settled right down at a low whuffle from Cookie.

"I think you're exactly right. This is a good chance for me to help out a friend. Billy thinks I'll be able to get business interruption insurance to cover expenses while I rebuild the clinic. So, I can slow down, do things right, and help others along the way—and I'm as excited about that as I am about you and me," he said. "We've already been through the storm. Everything else from here is just getting back to business as usual—or in our case, business as unusual, I guess. We're never going back to what 'usual' was between us before the storm."

"Never," Becca agreed.

Ross turned her way, and Becca met him in the middle with a kiss to seal the promise.

9

$\mathcal{I}$n the time that Ross spent in San Antonio, the recovery efforts in Port Provident began to pick up speed--just as Becca and Ross had predicted at the start of the week. Several restaurants and businesses re-opened for business, including the grocery store and one of Becca's favorite places to eat, Huarache's Mexican Restaurant on Gulfview Boulevard. Even the dusk-to-dawn curfew had been lifted.

Life had begun to feel like the hurricane was shrinking ever smaller in the rearview mirror. Even Polly was back to her old self, and Becca made it her mission to keep the sweet older dog near a bowl of water daily so that her medical condition stayed as managed as possible.

Becca bought a Bible on an impulse after seeing it in a side display at the grocery store. On Friday night, she decided to bring it with her to a table on the deck at Huarache's. She wanted a nice basket of chips and some salsa on the side so she could enjoy the breeze, the sight of the waves, and the peace she'd recently found in her heart.

She was even about to do something she'd never done in her adult life. Yesterday, Diana Peoples stopped by the shelter to check in on Becca and see if there was anything more the Peoples Family Foundation or Peoples Property Group could do for her. While they talked, Diana invited Becca to come with her to Sunday morning services at First Provident Church. She assured Becca that the service would be small and informal since so many members remained off the island and much of the main sanctuary had sustained damage.

It wouldn't seem like church at all—just time among her fellow Port Providenters learning a message of hope from God's word.

When Diana put it that way, it didn't seem so stuffy or scary. Becca agreed—and surprised herself by looking forward to it.

Becca settled herself in at a table on the corner of the patio. There would be no one to block her view of the gulf or to disturb her as she flipped through the pages. Did one just start at the beginning and go through? Or, did one flip around and study what looked interesting? Becca hadn't really ever thought about actually reading a Bible.

Shrugging, she opened to page one and decided that was as good a place as any to start.

After a while, Becca heard a rustle as someone leaned from the outside against the rail surrounding the patio.

"So, you decided to get in touch with your heritage?" The voice was raspy. It startled Becca, and she lost track of the page she'd been reading.

A woman with short, dirty-blonde hair crossed her arm on the rails. Wrinkles had settled in around the corners of her mouth and creased the skin to the sides of the eyes.

But Becca knew those eyes.

She saw them every morning when she looked in the mirror.

"Mom?" Becca's heart pounded and pushed the single syllable out of her throat.

"In the flesh." Darla Collins raised her arms to the sky dramatically. Her bra strap stuck out from the sides of the worn tank top that had probably once been a very hot shade of pink. Now it was lukewarm, to say the least.

Salsa burned Becca's throat. It met a wave of pure bile coming straight up her esophagus. She battled to keep it all down. "What are you doing here?"

"Checking on you," she said with a brittle laugh. "I needed to know if my baby girl was okay after that hurricane."

"You're not even supposed to know I'm here." Becca scooted her chips and salsa a little to the left. She didn't want to talk to this woman. She didn't want to share her tortilla chips. She didn't want anything involving Darla.

"Beccabug, I hired a private investigator to find you. I've been so worried about you for so long."

Becca shook her head in disbelief. "You paid someone money to find me?"

"Why wouldn't I? You're my only child, Becca. I wanted to see you. Come on, can't I sit down and talk to you?"

That answer was easy. "No."

"Rebecca Marie. Are you reading the Bible? Do you think Jesus would want you to just shut your mother out like that?"

Becca stared down at the basket of chips, wishing they were feathers so she could put on wings and just fly away like a seagull. Why was someone asking her questions about Jesus? She hadn't had this Bible open for more than fifteen minutes. She didn't know anything about Jesus, really, except what she'd learned and tried to forget from Bess' attempts at teaching her two decades ago.

She did, however, remember Diana's words about love. Becca knew she didn't love Darla. Not really even one bit. But if what Darla said was true…then maybe Darla had changed. Maybe Darla had found some love in her heart for her only daughter.

Someone wouldn't hire a private investigator for any other reason, right? Someone wouldn't spend the time and the money after close to twenty years with almost no contact unless something in your heart and mind had changed, right? And someone wouldn't mention Jesus unless they'd found a reason to believe.

Becca tried to think about it from that perspective.

She pushed out the other chair at the table with her left foot.

"So, I can sit there, Beccabug? It's okay?"

Becca shrugged. It was hard to commit fully to what was happening, but hopefully, Jesus would understand the struggle that raged in her heart right now and wouldn't hold a raised shoulder or a pushed chair against her.

Darla opened the gate to the patio and walked on in. As usual, her skirt was too short, and her heels were too high. Becca guessed some things would never change.

Her mother sat delicately on the edge of the chair and scooted it closer to the table, laying her clutch purse directly in front of her. "Now, isn't this nice? We can catch up."

Becca picked up a chip and crunched deliberately before pursuing the conversation further. She didn't exactly know what to say. She wasn't about to give any details about her life to Darla until she felt more comfortable about this situation.

But Darla had said something that piqued her curiosity.

"What did you mean about getting in touch with my heritage?"

"Oh, that. Your father. He was Mexican. I can't stand greasy Mexican food, so you have to get it from him."

"Ricky wasn't Mexican, Mom. He was from Chicago."

Darla's laugh squeaked as it came out her nose instead of her throat. "Ricky wasn't your dad. Your dad was a guy named Gerardo Jimenez. He went to jail before you were born. I only saw him once after that."

The chip Becca had been chewing on suddenly turned to sandpaper in her mouth. Just like that, her world shattered a little. "How could you not have told me?"

"Does it make some kind of a difference?"

Becca watched as Darla's spine noticeably stiffened.

"Why wouldn't knowing who my father is make a difference? You're telling me that something I've believed my whole life was a lie. Ricky was a total loser, and I hated him, but this…this…I don't…"

Darla crisscrossed her hands on top of the purse. "That's why I'm here, Beccabug. I want to come clean. I need to make it up to you."

"Make what up to me? You weren't a mother to me. You locked me in a closet so you could do drugs with your friends. Your boyfriend beat me almost unconscious because I wet my bed when I was five. The state took me away from you and sent me to live with strangers."

Her breath came short, and her chest began to pound. "How could you ever make that up to me?"

"Bad choice of words." Darla reached out and tapped the cover of Becca's new Bible. "But Jesus forgives me. I hope you will too."

Becca's chest stayed tight, like the throes of the asthma attacks she used to have when she was younger. And in her head, thoughts of Ross raced around. Oh, how she wished he was here. He'd know what to do, what to say back.

He knew Jesus. He'd have a Plan A and a Plan B and maybe even a Plan C.

She didn't have a plan, and she didn't have any kind of relationship with Jesus beyond being acquaintances. She was just a woman at a table with a book of stories she was still trying to decide whether or not she believed in.

It seemed as though her mother thought her daughter had it all together. Her mother kept bringing up Jesus. Becca couldn't let on that she was a Jesus-fake.

Becca needed her mother to know she'd grown up just fine without her. She needed Darla to realize she'd become a strong, independent woman regardless of all the obstacles Darla had thrown in her way. If she could just give Darla what she was looking for, maybe Darla would get out of town quickly and leave Becca to the life she'd created.

There. She'd drawn up Plan A. She'd just play along—kind of like she did when she was a kid. Long ago, she'd quickly figured out that with Darla, it was easier to do or say anything that matched what Darla was looking for. That kept you out of more trouble.

Surely that old trick would still work. She'd just tell Darla what she wanted to hear, then Darla would leave.

Against the better judgment of every one of the trillions of cells in her body, Becca's mouth had blurted out "you can just stay with me" when Darla asked if Becca knew of a place to stay because it seemed like every hotel on the island that was open was filled with contractors or people displaced from their homes.

If she hadn't needed one foot to work the gas and the other to work the clutch in order to drive her car home, Becca would have kicked herself repeatedly during the trip from Huarache's to her apartment.

Darla talked non-stop. Becca barely listened. She didn't want to be tempted to reply. Once they got in the elevator to the top floor of the Hinckman-Mercer building, Darla's chatter literally bounced off the four walls of the small metal rectangle.

It gave Becca a headache—which, she noted, matched up nicely with the overwhelming sense of nausea that had not left the pit of her stomach since she realized who the blonde lady trying to get her attention was.

"Oh, so this is where you live?" Darla practically squealed as Becca unlocked the door and walked inside.

"For now, at least." She didn't want to get into the specifics of her living arrangement here. Her reply signaled that it was temporary, and that was the honest truth. More details were just unnecessary at this point.

Darla threw back the curtains that framed the large windows at the center of the living room. "And look at this view! So much water. You're not in Wisconsin anymore, girlfriend."

"Nope."

"Beccabug, I think you're holding back on me. You're being awful quiet." Darla turned slightly as she fingered the thick tan cloth of the curtains embroidered with a rich, gold thread.

No one needed to hire a private detective to figure *that* one out. "Well, Mom, you have to admit this is awkward. We haven't spoken in decades, and then you show up at a restaurant I'm eating at, tell me my real dad is Hispanic, and ask me if I know Jesus. It's all a little strange, to say the least. Why are you really here?"

Becca knew her tone had gone from flat to harsh in a matter of seconds, but she couldn't hide how she felt.

A sob escaped Darla's lips. Tears rolled down each cheek, cutting through the thick makeup. "You've got to believe me. I've been wrong. I've learned. I want to get to know you."

She stumbled on the rug as she walked to the couch, wiping away tears. Darla sat on the edge of the couch heavily, then patted the cushion near her. "Can you just come sit with me?"

Becca thought of all the tears this woman had made her shed. Scared tears as a child. Lonely tears as a teenager. She wasn't sure that she wanted her mother in her apartment at this moment. But one thing she did know with great certainty was there had been enough tears.

She hesitated, then put one foot in front of the other and found her way to the couch.

She looked at that cushion. Becca realized she had the opportunity to break the cycle, to dry the tears. If not here, where? If not now, when?

Slowly, she lowered herself onto the cushion. She couldn't stop herself from defensively crossing her legs and her arms, but she *was* sitting, as requested. Becca had made the move she needed to make, and she felt as though she'd made the right choice—even though it was one of the hardest choices she'd ever pushed herself to make.

"I guess you should just start at the beginning," Becca said, her throat almost raw with the words. She looked at the clock as Darla began to speak. Becca knew she was in for a late night. She hoped she was doing whatever Jesus would have told her to do She hadn't turned enough pages in that Bible to know for sure.

She hoped love would be enough to cover the road she knew she was about to walk.

Late Monday afternoon, Ross and his rental car reached the top of the causeway. Boats still lay lifeless on the side of the road, marsh grass twisted into every link of chain link fences, and debris was piled everywhere. Still, it felt good to be home.

It felt good to be back on the same island as Becca.

He'd only talked to her a few times while he'd been gone, and hadn't been able to get through to her in several days. Cell phone service was once again restored in Port Provident, but to label it anything other than spotty and infrequent would be overselling the network's capabilities.

Naturally, as soon as that thought crossed his mind, his phone rang —presumably just to prove him wrong.

"Figures," Ross muttered as he punched the button on the face of his smartphone and connected the call. "Dr. Reeder."

"Hey, Ross, it's Billy. I've got an update for you on the insurance claim. Do you have a second?"

"Sure, Billy. I'm just driving back into town from a few days doing some veterinary work in San Antonio."

"You've got some opportunities for side work?"

Billy's question seemed strange. It made Ross wonder just where this call was headed. "Not work, *per se*—more of a volunteer trip."

"Okay, well, if you can get a few side jobs, you might want to. I've got your car claim straightened out. That check will be cut at the end of next week. Everything is still moving forward on the rehab and claim on the clinic itself. I think I've even got everything straightened out on your rental equipment. But your business interruption insurance has been denied."

"Wait, what? I don't have a business to operate. It's definitely interrupted. So how does that get denied?"

The sound of a deep breath crackled through the phone. "Well, that coverage is part of the windstorm policy."

"And a hurricane is a storm largely made up of wind." Ross knew he sounded like a smart-aleck, but he couldn't help it. This news was confusing.

"Right. But it's also got a lot of water. And there are only about five businesses I know of that aren't in this boat, so believe me, you're not alone. I have to deliver this news to about thirty of my policyholders today—which I'm really not looking forward to. But long story short, they're denying all claims because they're saying the event that caused the interruption of your business was actually the water swamping the power grid and taking everything offline, not anything related to wind."

Ross felt his eyes begin to roll back in his head. "That's weak, Billy."

"I know, man. But that's insurance. There are about four of us in town who will be going to the state insurance board in Austin in the next week or so to fight this on behalf of our clients. But for now, I have to advise you to not plan on having those funds coming in."

They wrapped up the conversation and Ross drove the rest of his way through the streets of Port Provident on some kind of auto-pilot.

If having an open, functioning clinic was Plan A, having adequate insurance coverage to tide him over in the event of an emergency was Plan B. Now he was looking at needing a Plan C.

Ross couldn't even begin to start putting the pieces of that puzzle together right now.

The sound of Becca's voice, teasing him about all his planning tendencies, ran through his mind. *Becca.* That's what he needed right now.

Becca.

If he could see her, talk this through with her, he knew everything would work itself out.

He just needed to spend some time with the person he'd come to think of as his partner in this whole crazy rebuilding mess. Everything else would get sorted.

Ross drove by the shelter but didn't see Becca's car. So, he drove downtown and there, he saw her car parked in the spot she'd come to prefer. He parked his rental car in the public lot across the street from Becca's building and took the elevator to the top floor. He knocked at the door to Becca's apartment and waited for the door to open, but it stayed shut. He didn't even hear the noise of feet or paws behind the door.

He knocked again.

Just when he was about to give up, the door opened a small distance.

"Yes?"

Ross didn't recognize the blonde woman or the husky voice. "Is Becca here?"

He couldn't put his finger on what was going on. All he knew was he didn't like it. It didn't seem like Becca to have someone else open her door like this.

"She's not available."

The hair on the back of Ross' neck prickled. Call it a sixth sense, call it a gut reaction, call it the voice in the back of his head…whatever it was, he heard it loud and clear.

"I need to talk to her." He put on his best Army officer tone of voice.

The woman slid the door closed a little. "I told you, she's not available."

Ross threw his hand against the door and pushed it back. The woman stumbled, but he didn't care. He had to get to Becca. He had to find out what was going on. He gave the door another shove—just enough to open it to a width he could fit through.

All the training the Army instilled him came back in a flash. He went on the defensive. He acted.

The blonde took two backward steps and looked at Ross with red anger in her eyes. "Becca! Call the police. Someone is trying to break in!"

"Becca. I am not breaking in!" Ross shouted, loud enough that he could be heard no matter where she was. "Where are you?"

He didn't see her in the central living area. If she was here, she must be back in the bedroom. Ross' heart began to pound. He needed to see Becca like he never thought possible.

He needed to see her now.

He needed to know she was okay.

And he needed to know what was going on.

He put his hand on the doorknob to the bedroom. The woman came up and slapped at his hand.

"You will not disturb her!" She tried to get physical with him, grabbing at his arm.

As a rule, he didn't treat women with anything other than the utmost respect, but Ross was about to break some rules.

"Becca!" He shouted as he opened the door. "It's Ross, Becca. Everything's going to be okay."

Becca sat on the bed, legs crossed, with a book open in front of her. Tears fell over the curve of her left cheek. Ross rushed to the side of the bed and wrapped her in his arms.

"What's going on here?" His voice quickly retreated back from alarm a more usual tone.

She wriggled a bit and tried to sit up straight. "So… I guess you've met my mom."

The blonde woman leaned against the doorframe. Her eyes still focused on him like the red dot of a laser. The color, the focus, the intensity. It was all there, and he couldn't make sense of any of it.

"Your mom? From Wisconsin?"

The woman turned off her laser eyes and turned a softer gaze on Becca. "Who is this, Rebecca?"

"This is my…" Becca hesitated, flicking a glance up at Ross' face.

Ross continued to hold her. He'd never felt so protective of anyone in his life. "I'm her boyfriend. Dr. Ross Reeder."

All things considered, Ross had no interest in extending his hand for a polite shake. He already knew enough about this woman. He didn't need any more introduction.

A pair of dark eyebrows raised almost to the fringe of blond hair on the woman's forehead. "A doctor?"

"Doctor of Veterinary Medicine. That's what the diploma says." Ross couldn't seem to get his dander back down.

"Oh, so not like a real doctor. I thought there was a hospital here."

"There is. And I am a real doctor. A Doctor of Veterinary Medicine. I also served this country honorably in the United States Army and did a tour of duty in Iraq. Anything else you need to know?"

Ross waited for Becca to tell him he'd pushed too far. She didn't, but she also didn't move a muscle. She kept one finger on the book in front of her and otherwise allowed her body weight to be supported entirely in Ross' arms.

He didn't know exactly what to do here, so he was willing to follow her lead. But he *would* protect her.

"Mom, Ross is the best vet on this island. He is very much a real doctor to his patients, many of whom come to him from our shelter." Becca's tone sounded almost mousey, but Ross felt gratitude at the heartfelt sentiment behind the words.

"Either way, you just need some time by yourself. Your young man can come back later."

Ross turned his back away from Becca's mother so he could speak directly to Becca. "I came by because I wanted to talk to you about San Antonio and some things. I can wait if you need me to. But I need to know you're okay right now. I need to know what's going on."

"Mom, please give us a minute. Close the door behind you."

The blonde bounced off the door frame and started to move forward into the bedroom, instead of backward, as Becca had requested. Becca held up a hand.

"Mom, I need you to go into the living room and close the door behind you."

Finally, Ross heard a spark of spunk in Becca's voice. He was glad to hear the Becca he recognized.

The woman opened and closed her mouth wordlessly three times, then realized Becca wasn't changing her mind. She walked out slowly and closed the door with a controlled slam, as a way of demonstrating one last form of displeasure.

As soon as the door closed, Ross dropped his arms and squatted down so that he could be eye-to-eye with Becca. He spoke quietly because he didn't trust her mother to not be listening to every word through a crack in the door.

"Beck, what on earth is going on?"

"She came to make amends." Becca's voice sounded flatter than a crepe.

Ross couldn't accept that as a satisfactory answer, not after everything Becca had said about her history with her mother. "But why? How? What could she possibly say to you that you'd want to hear? You got on a bus as a teenager to put as much distance between you and your childhood as possible."

"She said she hired a private investigator to find me. She brought this book with baby pictures. She gave me information about my real dad—get this. Her boyfriend wasn't my dad. I'm even half-Hispanic. I never knew." Becca flipped through a couple of pages in the old album with three-by-five photographs stuck on the pre-glued pages. Some had discolored, others had faded. But there was no mistaking it—the little girl on the pages was Becca. Ross felt as though he was looking at a small time machine.

"I don't have any pictures from when I was a baby. And then of course, when I was in foster care, there's basically no record of those years. It's always been like the first years of my life only existed in my head. But look at these, Ross. Look at me."

A single, salty tear landed with a splat on Becca dressed up as a clown for Halloween. She looked to be about two.

"I didn't want to give her a chance. But I have to, Ross. I just have to." The words floated into the space between them.

Ross' heart tugged sharply as he looked at the photos and listened to Becca's words. Intellectually, he understood exactly what she was saying. It made perfect sense. But something about the woman's demeanor didn't add up to him.

"You know I'll always support you, Becca. But I'm also here to defend you, if it comes to that."

He knew the last part of his statement meant that he couldn't completely let his guard down, but all that was better left unspoken for now.

"Let's change the subject." The shadow fell from her face, and he saw the Becca he'd grown so used to. "How was San Antonio?"

"Good. There were a number of cases at the ranch that needed me. Everyone's taken care of now. How's Polly doing? I'm going to swing by the shelter and pick up Cookie on my way back to my place. Thanks for taking care of him for a few days."

She closed the book in front of her. "No problem. Polly's doing great—and I think much of it is due to the presence of her pal Cookie. He's almost as much of a dog whisperer as you are."

Ross couldn't help but laugh. "Maybe I should get him a white coat for around the clinic. A Lab in a lab coat."

"That would totally work," Becca said. "I think it would suit his studious personality well."

"Well, it'll have to wait until I get some income again. That's the other thing. Billy called and said that almost all of the business interruption claims in town are being denied—mine included. I'm going to have to look for some way to make basic food-and-bill-paying money while the clinic is being rebuilt."

"Like what?"

"I don't know. I'll think of something."

"That's your specialty." She tilted her head up and gave him a short peck on the lips.

The kiss was sweet, but not at all what he'd been hoping for as he'd thought of Becca for most of the drive between San Antonio and Port Provident. He'd missed her a great deal.

But it seemed a lot had changed in his few days off the island— almost as quickly as Hurricane Hope had turned his world upside down to begin with.

That perfunctory kiss said it all. And Ross didn't like the language it chose to speak.

10

*B*ecca hadn't seen much of Ross during the last two weeks. He still stopped in at the shelter every morning to check on the residents. He spent his afternoons in Houston helping a veterinarian friend on the south side of town who had a thriving practice.

For her part, Becca spent her afternoons trying to reunite the animals who had been brought into the Port Provident Animal Shelter with their families as the residents flowed back to the island from their storm-imposed exile. Other animals were surrendered to the shelter's care as their families realized that their new realities did not allow them to care for their pets in the way they used to before the storm.

Becca's heart tore over each one of these surrenders, but having lived through every minute of the storm and seeing the state of Port Provident every day, she couldn't sit in judgment on any of the owners. Instead, she took her heartbreak for these furry friends and pledged her energy to finding them the best new forever homes she possibly could.

Late last week, the president of the Port Provident Chamber of Commerce had stopped by the shelter. She was interested in having a ribbon-cutting event and inviting media to come out and see the Port Provident Animal Shelter as a shining example of the positive steps, the rebirth, going on in Port Provident. Enthusiastically, Becca agreed.

She was proud of the work she and Ross had done—and deep down inside, she hoped it might inspire some people to donate to the shelter.

It was tough to be a non-profit when everyone on the island needed a hand-up right now. Despite the progress made daily, that would probably continue to be the situation for non-profits in this community for months to come.

Now, today was the day for the shelter's coming out party and Becca hurriedly ran around, taking care of the last-minute details.

The bell over the front door jingled, and Polly gave a welcoming *woof!* from her spot near Becca's feet.

"You've got a key to the back door, silly." She smiled as Ross came in. It was good to see him in the middle of the day. She'd missed having him around.

Cookie followed behind his owner, and Becca heard Polly's tail go *thwap-thwap-thwap* against the wall in joyous canine greeting as she sighted and smelled her friend.

"Too many cars in the lot. I had to park down the street and walk." He gave her a side-hug and a kiss on the top of the head. "You ready for this? I counted four TV station trucks out there."

"Really?" Becca rushed to the front window and looked out. "My goodness. I can't believe it."

"You've done great work here, Becca. It shouldn't surprise you that people want to come out here. They want to see and celebrate things like this."

Becca teased him with a pointing finger. "This is as much your work as it is mine."

"Not really. The shelter is your passion. It has been for years."

She caught a hint of hesitation in his voice. "What is it?"

"I got another call from San Antonio."

Clearly, there was more to it than just a need for a helping hand with some vet care. "And?"

"Gina's retiring. She wants to spend time with her grandkids in Colorado. And she's asked me to buy her out and take over the ranch."

Becca felt her eyes stretch so wide that her eyelids almost began to hurt. "She wants you to move to San Antonio?"

"Well, yeah. She'd still own the ranch, but I'd own the business. So that would be part of it."

"A big part of it." Becca crossed her arms over her chest.

Her mother appeared around the corner. "Becca, the news station wants to talk to you."

"Ross, we need to finish this conversation, but first let's go talk to the TV people." Becca ran her fingers through her hair. Butterflies dipped and waved in her stomach. She'd never been on TV before.

Darla stepped between Becca and Ross. "Not you. They just want Becca."

"Mom, Ross and I did this together. He can come."

"Rebecca, I've been talking to the reporter for the last few minutes. This is your moment. I'm sure Dr. Reeder can occupy himself for a bit." Darla placed a hand on Becca's shoulder and scooted her the few paces out the door without any room for further conversation.

Becca looked back over her shoulder, but Darla kept pushing and talking. There wasn't a chance to do things differently. She felt uncomfortable going to speak to a reporter about the shelter without Ross, but her mother pushed her to go alone.

She kept reminding herself that the greatest of these was love. She had committed to treating her mother with love, to doing what she needed to do so her mother would find what she was looking for and then go back to Wisconsin.

Ross understood love. He'd understand what she was trying to do. Becca just needed to peel her mother's shadow off her for five minutes so she could explain it to him.

A crowd of people surrounded Becca for the next hour. Two people chatted up Ross. Mentally, keeping up with those small conversations drained him. The only person he wanted to talk to was Becca, and she was the one person in the room he couldn't get near.

Even Polly and Cookie hung back from the crowds, laying down on their large beds behind the front desk.

Ross looked at his watch. It was four-thirty in the afternoon, and things had become as bright as the shining sun. He could still get everything settled today.

He snapped his fingers and Cookie popped up from his bed. The dog readjusted his tennis ball, gave Polly a parting sniff and lumbered over to Ross.

As he neared the front door, Ross paused. Becca's dark hair fell straight over her shoulders like a waterfall. Her smile was bright and her eyes locked on the city councilwoman she was talking to. She looked beautiful and strong—the scene in front of him was the essence of the girl he'd fallen in love with.

Except for the presence of one over-tanned blonde woman standing next to her.

Ross didn't quite understand the hold Darla Collins had been able to lock around her daughter in just a matter of days. He didn't understand Becca's thought process of sweeping decades of abuse and abandonment by the wayside.

The woman across the room *looked* like the Becca he'd fallen for. But inside, she was no longer that woman. She wasn't even the woman he'd sparred with in board meetings. This Becca barely had time to talk to him anymore. This Becca was an imposter.

Or maybe…maybe she was the real Becca. His heart squeezed at the thought, and a feeling like a dark, black cloud settled just over his shoulders.

Either way, Ross figured, he'd never really know.

It took Becca about two hours to break down the tables and chairs from the afternoon's event. She'd swept floors and mopped them spotless. She placed the last few paper cups and soda cans in a large black trash bag, tied the yellow handles tightly shut, and dragged it out the back door to the large trash can at the edge of the back sidewalk.

As she walked back toward the shelter, the picnic table on the patio caught her eye. One tea light sat askew on the ground beside the far bench.

Becca walked over and leaned down to pick it up. She rolled the small cylinder of white wax between her fingertips and closed her eyes, remembering a night with a sea of stars in the sky and flickering flames on the ground.

Her head began to pound just over the right temple. Becca never dreamed Darla would have stayed this long. Darla didn't know the meaning of the word 'roots.' She'd always been restless and self-centered. When Becca had first pieced together her plan amid the shock of Darla's surprise return, she'd assumed that by telling Darla what she wanted to hear, her mother would move on to the next thing quickly.

That's how Darla had acted for as long as Becca could remember. But instead, Becca's attention seemed to be giving her mother more reasons to stay. And the longer Darla stayed, glued to Becca's side, the more distant Becca felt from Ross. She couldn't get any time alone with him, and she couldn't explain things thoroughly with her mother listening to every word.

She'd missed Ross the last few weeks. She missed the man who would go to the trouble of setting up a magical four-star evening for her just because she'd never had one. She missed the arms that held her steady against her darkest fears as a hurricane moved in. She missed the gentle reasoning of a man who made a faith-filled life real to her simply because of the sincerity of how he lived. She missed getting lost in his kisses.

And most of all, she missed knowing she had a partner, someone who understood her work and her vision and would be there beside her during the long days of rebuilding to come.

It dawned on Becca that she was completely alone right now. Her mother was back at the apartment. She'd claimed her feet were sore from standing in heels at the Chamber event and she needed to soak them in a hot bath.

If she hurried, Becca could have all the animals fed and supplied with fresh water and ready for the night in about thirty minutes. And then she could stop by Ross' place before heading to her own.

Perfect. Ross would be proud—she'd come up with a good course of action, and Becca was going to see to it that she executed it perfectly. No Plan B needed here.

The sky was settling into the dark as Becca climbed the stairs alongside Ross' garage. Polly ambled up each wooden stair, just a half-step behind Becca. It still amazed Becca how Polly had seamlessly become a part of her life in such a short time. She hadn't heard from the McCaw family since they boarded the bus on the afternoon Hurricane Hope came to town, and Becca sometimes wondered if they would be like the thousands of other Port Provident residents who were settling in new towns and cities and would never return to the island.

At the door, she took a deep breath to steady herself, although she didn't know why her veins suddenly shook alive with nervous adrenaline. She was going to see Ross—the man who she'd found she could talk to about anything.

She'd just explain what was going on and then everything would be fine. Back to normal...or whatever normal had become in the wake of a hurricane.

Becca raised her hand and rapped on the door three quick times.

The door swung open, and Ross stood a half step back. "Hey, Becca. Is Polly okay?"

"Yeah, she's right here." Becca pointed just behind her, where Polly was barely visible due to the darkness of the sky.

"Good. Does one of the other animals need me?"

He sounded genuinely concerned for the animals' welfare, but Becca couldn't figure out why he didn't invite her in.

May as well just bite the bullet. "Everyone's fine. Mind if I come in?"

Ross scratched the top of his head. "No, I guess not. I mean, sure."

He didn't exactly roll out the red carpet, but Becca took advantage of the invitation and stepped inside. Polly followed behind and immediately walked over to Cookie's crate and made herself at home near the front opening.

"Did everything go well today?" Ross sat down on the edge of the futon.

"It did. I got to see some of the coverage on the news as I was cleaning up. I hope that we'll be able to use this as a springboard for both adoptions and donations. This was definitely good publicity."

"Good. I'm glad." His tone was flat, almost as though he didn't care. But that didn't make sense to Becca. She knew he cared about the shelter and the animals who lived there.

"I looked for you after things wrapped up. I didn't see you anywhere." She placed her purse carefully on the edge of the kitchen counter, and as she did so, a stack of cardboard boxes caught her eye. "You going somewhere?"

Ross looked at the stack of boxes against the wall in the kitchen and another pile behind Cookie's crate before looking down at his hands. "San Antonio."

"Wait. What?" Becca didn't understand. "You just got back from San Antonio. You're leaving again?"

He shifted position on the futon, seeming to search for the right place to start, but once he began to speak, his voice was calm and measured. "I told you that Gina approached me about taking over operations at the ranch. I called her back this afternoon and accepted the offer."

The words felt like a punch to the chest. She lost her breath for a moment and couldn't seem to catch any new air. "But we were going to talk more about that. You're leaving Port Provident? You've made the decision?"

In her head, another phrase screamed—*"You're leaving me?"*—but she couldn't get it out into the open.

"I don't have a job, and I've got bills to pay. I need to eat. I'm blessed to have an opportunity come to me that gives me the chance to continue my veterinary work and my passion for working with dogs who've worked with our soldiers."

"So...Plan B?" Becca couldn't even string together complete sentences. Here she'd sat on the back patio only an hour before, thinking about the partnership between the two of them, and now her so-called partner was leaving.

"Becca, look. You've got the shelter back open now. You got great publicity today—and as you said yourself, it's going to drive financial support and adoptions. And your mother is back in your life. The pieces of your puzzle are falling back into place."

No, no they weren't. The pieces of her heart were breaking and falling to the floor. She'd always thought Darla Collins was a cynic when it came to men, but for the first time in her life, she realized that maybe her mother was right.

Becca had let her guard down for Ross. She'd let him into her once fiercely-independent life. And it hadn't gotten her anywhere, even though she knew why things had come to this moment.

Pride welled in her throat and choked off any words she might have been able to use. If she stayed here and explained what she'd originally come to explain to Ross, she'd just look like a fool.

Ross had already made up his mind to leave. No matter how much she felt she'd changed since she showed up on his front porch with a Labrador retriever, she still wasn't the type to beg someone to stay. She never would be. Besides he was right—he needed a job, needed money coming in. This was an opportunity for him to do that and do what he loved. Trying to explain herself would only muddy the waters and make all this harder.

But he was wrong. His pieces were coming together. Hers weren't. Even so, she needed to let him do what he'd decided was best for him.

That's what love did, right? She was trying to live according to love these days—and it was all going terribly wrong. This is why she didn't believe in all that Bible silliness. It didn't work for people like her.

Love wasn't the greatest of these, it was the traitor of these. It had built her hopes up and now was letting her down. She'd tried to love Ross, and now he was leaving. She'd tried to love her mother, and now she couldn't get rid of her. The wrong person was going, and the wrong person was staying.

Love was exactly what she'd always assumed it to be. It wasn't great. It was a mess.

She felt the pieces of her heart gluing back together, like concrete pouring into a mold. It felt semi-soft now, but she knew it would harden shortly. Becca didn't need love. And she didn't need a bunch of religious nonsense, either.

"Well, then," she said, the dismissal tasting bitter on her tongue. She steeled herself to get through the next few sentences and then she'd be done and could move on. Just like Ross was doing. Moving. "Best of luck to you with your own puzzle pieces and Plan B."

He remained on the futon. Becca knew she'd remember how he looked in this moment forever. The way his dark blue T-shirt almost perfectly matched the dark denim of his jeans. The way the laces on his black Converse sneakers were tied lopsided. The way he sat so low that his knees were level with his shoulders.

The way his eyes searched her face, then looked away.

She'd never forget any of it.

～

Or how isolated she felt right now—all in the name of love.

Becca stalled on her way home. She went into the grocery store to pick up a freezer meal for lunch tomorrow. After the store, she decided to pull through for some French fries and a soda, since her favorite fast-food restaurant had re-opened this week.

Then, Becca pulled over into a parking space along Gulfview Boulevard and tried to watch the waves.

The salt dusted over the fries was no match for the salt that stung her eyes as she finally let her emotions have free run in the privacy of her car. She wouldn't be able to process her feelings once she got back to the apartment.

Darla would be there, waiting for her. First, Darla would dump on Becca about how much her feet hurt and how stressful it had been with all the people around at the event today. Then once she stopped talking long enough to notice Becca's feelings, Darla wouldn't rest until she'd needled every possible emotion out of her daughter and dispensed an unending stream of her own Darla-focused advice.

That wasn't love.

Love was patient, love was kind. She remembered that from sitting on the curb with Diana Peoples, who gave her more kind and caring advice in ten minutes than Darla Collins had imparted since the day Becca was born.

Love was holding someone through the night as a storm raged. Love was tea lights and four-star dinners under the stars. Love was giving your days and nights to renovate a shelter for the animals who needed care.

Love was Dr. Ross Reeder.

Love was what she felt for Ross. And now he was gone.

Love was gone.

She couldn't see any reason to stall any longer. It didn't matter what awaited her when she got back to the apartment. Love was gone, and it wasn't coming back.

She'd tried to show love to someone who had disappointed her for her entire life. And while that wasn't the wrong course of action, it took her away from growing love with someone who had shown his patience and kindness and faith and hope to her every single day since a hurricane named Hope came to town.

Hurricane Hope had brought faith and hope and love to her door, and she'd thrown it away.

"Oh, God…what did I do?" Becca rested her head on the upper curve of the steering wheel. "We don't talk a lot, but can you hear me? Are You there?"

A seagull landed on the hood of her car. Polly raised her head and gave a strong *woof!*

"Oh my gosh, You are there." She knew in her heart that bird was meant for her. She heard a flap of wing and a squawk of beak, and peace settled over her. "I've gotten it all so wrong. Just show me love. That's all. Just show me love. I don't want to get it wrong again."

She took a deep, fortifying breath as she raised back into a sitting position. As she pressed a pedal and shifted the car into gear, she took one last look at the waves rolling from the horizon to the shore. They rose and bobbed and crested and started the process over and over and over before they ever rolled up on the sand. They didn't get to shore the first time. But they did regroup and rise again, and eventually, they arrived at their destination.

Becca would get where she was going too. She knew it in her heart. She'd found the meaning of love. And even if it took her trying, trying again, she'd never stop learning and trying to get it right.

She put the car in drive and pressed down the gas. Forward was the only way she knew to go now. She would always have Ross to thank for that, even though it hurt terribly to admit she no longer had him in her life.

As she walked into the apartment, it took Becca a few minutes to process the scene in front of her. Darla was resting on the couch, holding some kind of sleek black rectangle in her hand. On the table sat stacks of open catalogs.

"What's that?"

"A tablet. It was delivered today. And then a nice young man on the customer service line at your cell phone provider helped me get it all set up. Since the Internet is still spotty here, I can just connect online through the data plan."

Becca stood fixed in the entryway. "I don't understand. My cell phone provider? How did you find out who my cell phone provider is? My phone is tied to the shelter's business account."

"I know," Darla said, matter-of-factly. "I found all the paperwork when I was filing in the office a few days ago. They have really good customer service. Most cell phone providers don't, you know."

Becca didn't care about other cell phone providers. All she cared about right now was finding out what Darla was up to. "My cell phone plan has a specific amount of minutes and data on it every month. I work for a non-profit. My plan won't support surfing the Internet on a tablet. And my budget won't support buying a tablet. We're recovering from a hurricane right now, in case you hadn't noticed. Who bought the tablet?"

Darla batted her eyes sheepishly. "Well, I just had them add it to your account."

"You did what?" Becca practically spat out the words. "A tablet is an IT expenditure, according to the rules I work under. And IT expenditures have to be approved by the board. I could lose my job, Darla."

"You're not going to lose your job, Rebecca. Just keep that vet happy in bed. He's on your board. I've seen how he looks at you. He's not going to fire you over a couple of hundred dollars."

Becca needed a stopwatch to time how fast her jaw dropped. "I'm not sleeping with Ross Reeder! What on earth, Mom? Just because that's the only way you know how to communicate with men...it does not mean I am the same as you. I have a legitimate job. I earn a real paycheck. I've carried my own load for more than ten years."

"Is that what you think of me?" Darla changed positions. No longer lounging back on the cushions, she now leaned slightly forward—like a cat waiting to pounce.

Becca couldn't answer that entirely without knowing the answer to another question first. She looked around Darla's immediate area, and suddenly the pieces began to fit together. Unfortunately, they were very different pieces from the ones Ross spoke of earlier.

"Why are you here?" She put one hand on her hip, trying to keep her claws from totally coming out. "Why are you buying tablet computers and sitting surrounded by open furniture catalogs?"

"I wanted to know you. I told you that."

Becca narrowed her gaze. "Wrong answer. Why are you really here, Darla?"

"Rebecca Marie." Her mother put as much emphasis on the syllables as she could. "You are ruining a good evening. I had a great bubble bath and relaxed, and then I came in here and bought you some lovely new furniture for your new house and business. I was looking forward to showing it to you. We could have had a nice mother-daughter evening."

"You bought furniture? With what? For *where*?" Becca's heart began to pound. Her mind feared the worst. Would she be able to get everything canceled before the bills came in?

"Your insurance settlements will be here before everything's due. I opened some new credit cards for you—some of them even have six months or more to pay."

Becca demanded the names of the stores. Darla grudgingly shared them.

If she didn't suffer a stroke from the shock and fear and panic that Darla's actions had brought on, Becca knew she'd be able to survive just about anything.

"I get it now," Becca said slowly. "And I could kick myself for not seeing it earlier. You *did* hire a private investigator to find me. But you didn't do anything about it until after a hurricane, when you assumed I'd be in line for some big insurance settlement. You didn't want a relationship with me. You wanted someone to finance your lifestyle, the same as you always have."

"Now, Rebecca. That's a terrible thing to say. I love you, Beccabug."

Becca cut Darla off before she could say anything further. "That's not love. That's fraud. You changed contracts on behalf of my business. You opened credit cards in my name without my consent. You need to leave. Right now. If you're not gone in ten minutes, I'm calling the police, and I'm filing charges on you."

"But I love you, Becca!" Even though Darla didn't move, her face completely transformed. Her cheeks sunk, her lips dried out and the look in her eyes moved to somewhere far away.

She looked like the human version of the very fraud she'd just perpetrated on her daughter.

"Love is kind, Mother. You don't know love. I do."

$\mathcal{B}$ecca rolled over on the air mattress in the back room at the new animal shelter. She'd outfitted the small space with the basics to be a home-away-from-home. The fresh morning light streamed in through the small window on the back wall, washing over her face and making sure that she was up and facing the day—whether she'd wanted to be or not.

She'd spent most of the weekend on this air mattress, unable to spend time in her apartment. Every time she looked at the couch, she saw the moment when her mother's face changed and revealed the woman's true nature.

And every time she looked anywhere else, she remembered seeing the apartment for the first time with Ross.

So, instead of being alone with the memories that tormented her, she stayed here after hours, with the animals that needed her. Hearing the barks and yaps and meows all night long reminded her that in truth, she wasn't as alone as she felt. Polly stuck by Becca's side like a furry, drooling shadow. For that, Becca stayed grateful.

She'd seen what she'd thought of as love turned upside-down in the last few days. But Polly's companionship remained constant.

Somehow, it was as though the geriatric Labrador had always been there.

Becca got dressed and made the food and potty rounds for all of the animals in residence. With everyone settled for the rest of the morning, she headed to the front desk to return phone calls. A few adoption inquiries had come in yesterday.

As she began to dial, the bells on the front door chimed. Becca hung up the receiver and instead turned her attention to her in-person visitor.

"Welcome to the Port Provident Animal Shelter..." Her voice trailed off as she realized who stood in the waiting area. Eloise McCaw and her granddaughter.

Eloise leaned heavily on a metal walker. "We've come to collect Polly."

At the sound of the familiar voice, Polly's ears twitched and her tail wagged.

Becca drew up enough strength to give the dog a pat on the top of her flat head. "Go on, girl," she whispered in a halting tone.

Polly trotted around the side of the desk and took off running when she saw her family. Becca's heart sank at the sight of them embracing the gentle dog who'd meant so much to Becca since the storm. She had known thousands of dogs during her career, but none had captured her heart as thoroughly as Polly Wolly Doodle McCaw.

"I'm glad to see you've made it home safely," Becca said to the McCaws. "Welcome back to Port Provident."

The younger girl shook her head. "Well, we're not staying. Our apartment was completely wiped out and my mom worked at the Come Home Inn and Suites. Her job is gone until they rebuild. So, we're staying in San Antonio. My mom's already found a job there. Grandma and I only came back for the day to get Polly. We've missed her."

"Oh, yes, I understand." The words tore at Becca's throat like a cat on a scratching post. Never had a phrase felt so inadequate. "Polly is a special girl."

"Do we owe you anything?" Mrs. McCaw reached for her black leather purse.

Becca struggled to speak. "No, of course not. The pleasure has been all mine."

Suddenly, everything about Port Provident felt too small, too confining. Becca flipped the sign in the window to "closed," grabbed her key ring, locked the door behind her and just started walking. The island was twenty-seven miles long from the westernmost point to the easternmost tip. Becca knew she could walk the whole length and back again and still not have covered enough ground to give her mind time to sort out the jumble of thoughts that swirled in her mind like Hurricane Hope's most savage clouds.

So much pressure was building up in her head that her scalp started to hurt. She could feel the individual hairs where they attached through the skin.

Every footfall along her unplanned path echoed one word: failure.

She'd failed at everything lately. And now she was all alone. Everyone she cared about was in San Antonio. But there was no way she could move to San Antonio. And even if she did, what was the point?

Polly was someone else's dog.

And Ross would eventually become someone else's love.

How desperate would it be if she traveled halfway across Texas to live in the same city as a person and a dog that weren't even hers? No. Not an option. She needed the one thing Ross always advocated—a Plan B.

She kept her head bowed, counting the cracks in the sidewalk as she kept up her fast and furious pace. No good thoughts came to mind —no alternatives. Nothing that would give her direction for where to go next.

She knew God had sent her that seagull the other day to let her know He was listening. But she was too embarrassed even to try talking to Him. She couldn't possibly admit this mess to anyone other than herself.

She slowed as she reached an intersection and looked up to see what color the traffic light was on. Across the street, she saw First

Provident Church. Maybe He'd heard everything even though she hadn't uttered a word out loud?

In the parking lot stood the same white tent she'd visited with Ross the morning after the storm.

Her stomach growled at the memory. She'd just stop, grab a bottle of water and a banana and keep on with her head-clearing walk.

"Becca!" Diana Peoples' voice sounded full of joy. "How are you, dear? I saw the segment on the news. It turned out wonderfully. Have you gotten any good feedback?"

She pushed herself to make eye contact with Diana. It wouldn't be right to treat this kind woman with anything but the utmost respect. "We've gotten several calls about donations, and a company in Houston is interested in donating some prizes to the annual charity auction."

"Wonderful! I guess one day we'll have another board meeting and you can update us on where we stand. I think everyone is back on the island."

"Ross Reeder isn't. He moved to San Antonio."

Diana shook her head. "What? No, he didn't. I saw him this morning at the grocery store."

Becca slapped down the warming feeling in her heart. It didn't matter that Diana had seen Ross today. That was just temporary. He was moving, and *that* was the bottom line.

"Can you walk over to the chairs with me for a moment, Becca dear?" Diana gestured to the next tent over. "It's my break time."

Becca needed to get back to stepping over cracks in the sidewalk, but she couldn't say no to Diana. A few minutes wouldn't make much difference.

"Your eyes are red. What's wrong?" They walked side-by-side, and Diana slipped an arm around Becca's shoulder.

Becca didn't want to open up to God. She didn't want to open up to Diana. She didn't want to open up to anyone. She shook her head.

Diana sat in a white plastic lawn chair and patted the seat of an identical chair next to her. "I am not the type to pry, Becca. But I'm also not the type to leave a friend wiping away tears by herself."

And just like that, the words came bubbling out of Becca's mouth.

"Everyone's left. I misjudged everything. I got it all wrong, Diana. I don't know anything about love. I tried so hard after we talked here last time. You said the greatest thing was love. I tried to put it first. I gave the benefit of the doubt where I shouldn't have. I let someone leave because I thought that was supporting them, but I should have been honest and asked them to stay. Even the dog I've been taking care of has left me. I'm completely alone, and it's all my fault."

Diana patted Becca on the leg. "What do you mean you don't know anything about love?"

"I don't. I called the truth a lie and a lie the truth. I tried to do the right thing, and in the end, I did everything wrong."

"I see." Diana thought for a minute, then continued. "I remember that conversation we had. But there's more to what the Bible says about love than those verses. Luke tells us that we're to love our enemies. If you gave someone the benefit of the doubt—even if they turned out to lie to you, you've done what the Bible asks. So, you're okay there. And the Bible says over and over that we're to love one another. Do you know why?"

Becca sniffed and wiped her nose with a napkin she'd picked up in line. "No."

"Because God is love. So, if you know God, you know love." Diana picked up Becca's hand. "Do you know God, my dear?"

"I don't know if I do," she replied softly. "But I think I'd like to."

It felt strange to admit such a thing after years of calling the Bible a book of stories and nonsense.

"Well, that's easily remedied. Just bow your head and repeat after me."

It was easy enough for Becca to do as she'd been asked. Her head had been bowed in shame and embarrassment for days now. Diana walked her through a short prayer.

"And that's it," Diana said, raising her head and tapping Becca under the chin with two quick fingers, as a signal to do the same. "You know love. And I think you know you're in love with someone that I may have seen this morning."

"I do." Becca breathed the crisp early autumn air into her lungs.

"I've lived my whole life putting up defenses because people let me down almost from the day I arrived on earth. But since Hurricane Hope —with one exception—I've been around people like you and Ross, people who don't operate like that. You don't have defenses because you have a defender. People like my mother are different. They always had to have a defense because they were doing it all themselves. I see it now, Diana. But how do I make it up to Ross?"

Diana shrugged. "I don't know. But I do know you're not going to do it sitting in a chair in the First Provident parking lot. We know Ross was still in town two hours ago. We don't know how much longer that will be the case. I'd say you'd better hurry."

"Is that in the Bible too?" Becca stood up and looked for a trash can so she could throw away her banana peel.

"Well, not exactly. But we are called to run the race God has set before us. I think this is one of those times when you can take that teaching literally and figuratively."

Lightning sparked through Becca's body. Her feet were ready to move fast, but with a whole different motivation than they'd had just an hour before. Before she could go, though, there was one thing Becca knew she had to do.

She wrapped her arms around Diana and hugged her tightly. Diana reached her own arms around Becca's back and squeezed.

Diana was right. Becca knew love. Now it was time to take the first step—and as many more steps as it took until she reached Ross Reeder's front door.

"Get inside, Cookie." Ross opened the passenger-side door of the rented do-it-yourself moving truck.

It felt strange to be standing outside the place he'd lived and worked for several years, knowing this would be the last time he'd ever see it. The real estate agent would put a for-sale sign in the yard tomorrow morning, and if all went according to plan, they'd soon find an investor who wanted to fix it up and most likely flip the property.

Ross had been assured that kind of activity was happening in a flurry all over the island right now.

He heard the crunch of shoes on grass behind him and turned around to see who it was. Most of his neighbors hadn't returned home yet, so he hadn't gotten to say many goodbyes.

He figured he'd see Mr. Dalton from across the street, but instead Ross saw Becca.

Her long hair was once again pulled back into a low ponytail, and she wore a long-sleeved shirt from a long-ago Thanksgiving-themed fun run. Short jogging shorts revealed long legs that still bore the signs of an end-of-summer glow.

He couldn't take his eyes off her. But it broke his heart to stare. He'd loved the Becca he'd come to know, but she'd proven to him that the cliché was right. A leopard truly couldn't change spots. It wasn't her fault—too much change in a short period of time was hard for just about anyone to sustain.

He knew if there was a chance for her to restore her relationship with her mother, she needed to take it. But he greatly regretted what it had meant for the relationship they'd been building.

"Can I tell Cookie goodbye?" Becca took a step forward, then hesitated.

"Of course." Ross watched Becca scratch Cookie behind the ears, and his mind jumped to the way her fingers had threaded through his hair when they'd kissed and how those same fingers fit perfectly around his palm when they'd held hands.

He felt totally jealous of Cookie right now.

"Where's Polly?" Ross didn't see any signs of Becca's canine sidekick.

One corner of Becca's mouth twisted upward. "On her way to San Antonio with the McCaw family. They're moving there for good. Seems everyone I love is headed that way these days."

"Everyone you love? Your mom's moving to San Antonio?"

She looked down at the top of Cookie's head. "No, not her. I guess she's back in Wisconsin by now. I don't know."

"She's gone?" A little frisson of electricity sparked in Ross' heart.

"Yeah, I asked her to leave not long after you and I last talked—not long after I discovered she'd been basically stealing from me." She stopped scratching Cookie and looked squarely at Ross. "I'd heard that love basically covered all. I thought I was acting in love by giving her a second chance. I was wrong."

"So, your mom is gone, and Polly is gone?"

"Yes. And you're leaving too." She played with the edge of one sleeve.

"Well, I don't have much of a choice. I've got to keep the dog ranch up and running." He leaned against the door of the truck. "For a guy who has lived all over the world, this place feels like home. But there's nothing to keep me here. My practice is closed, and my money is tied up in insurance claims and selling this place."

Becca shifted from one foot to another. "What if you had a reason to stay here?"

"I'm listening." Even if she came out and said she was wrong and wanted to get back together, that wasn't going to pay the bills. He'd still have to go. But he could at least give Becca her say. She'd walked over here for some reason.

"Do the dogs have to live in San Antonio?"

"Well, no, I guess not. That's just where they are now. But people from all over the country come to Texas to adopt them, and the dogs themselves have lived all over the world."

"Then the Port Provident Animal Shelter would like to make you a formal proposal. We have recently moved into a building with a large yard and excess space. We are interested in purchasing this property from the Peoples Property Group to make it a long-term home for our animals waiting to find their forever families. But, in order to do that, we're going to need some additional revenue streams. We would like to offer the opportunity for both the veterinary practice of Dr. Ross Reeder and the Service Paws military dog placement program to relocate under our roof and partner with us to bring the most comprehensive animal health and rescue facility to Southeast Texas."

"You want me to move into the shelter building?"

"You and Cookie and all the other combat dogs."

Ross noticed Becca chewing on her lower lip, a sure sign that her outer confidence was covering up an inner insecurity.

"But why?"

"About six months ago, I was sitting in a meeting, and a guy told me I was taking the easy way out, and I needed to think creatively and consider all my options. This guy was always talking about a Plan B." She shrugged sheepishly. "It turns out that guy was pretty smart, and I'd been reading him wrong for years. So, I thought I'd be creative and offer you a Plan B. In fact, this idea sets up the Port Provident Animal Shelter to achieve its goals and operate in the black, and it does the same for the veterinary practice and Service Paws."

Ross couldn't keep a smile from spreading across his face. "When you put it that way, it's practically a Plan A."

A smile that matched Ross' own lit Becca's face. "Plan A-plus. Is it okay if I notify the board of the Port Provident Animal Shelter that we are going to have some new tenants? I know the president of the board personally."

"I think the arrangement should definitely be formalized, although this probably means the president of the board will need to resign due to the potential for conflict of interest."

Becca took three steps and closed the distance between them. The smile never wavered. "I can think of another position he can fill."

Ross leaned his head just above Becca's. "What's that?"

"I have an opening for a partner at work and in life. Would you be interested in assuming that role?"

He answered just before his lips brushed hers. "I think that sounds like a very good plan."

EPILOGUE

"*I* can't believe it, Ross! Look out the window! That's snow!" Becca practically squealed at the sight of the almost microscopic white flakes. She marveled as tiny snowflakes dancing above their island. "I haven't seen snow since I left Wisconsin!"

"You think we should head down to the beach and build a snowman?" Ross stood behind her and wrapped his arms around her waist. "I love seeing you this excited."

"It's nice to have something to be this excited about. You know, I used to think it wasn't possible."

Ross leaned down and nuzzled the spot at the juncture of her neck and shoulder. She shivered a little bit, and it wasn't just from the chill in the Christmas Eve air.

"Feeling like this, feeling free to be happy and to enjoy the everyday. I used to think life was something to be battled. I was always keeping my defenses up, always trying to keep the real me hidden away from everyone. It's how I survived those first years of my life, and it just became a pattern."

"I'm glad you're getting to be the real you. I like this Becca." He gently kissed her again. "Actually, that's not accurate. I love this Becca."

She turned her head parallel to her shoulder so she could look at this man who'd become her staunchest advocate, her sounding board, her partner in work, and her best friend in life.

"I love you too, Ross. And I know it sounds cheesy, but there's a part of me that loves Hurricane Hope. Without Hope, I never would have found my way to your front porch. We would never have walked to breakfast the next day at First Provident. And I never would have learned the true meaning of love—or found this with you."

His teeth shone in his smile as white as the twinkle lights on the Christmas tree in the corner of the room. "Nobody else is going to believe you when you say you love a hurricane, Beck. But I do. I believe there's always a plan, no matter what the circumstances seem to be."

"A Plan A or a Plan B?" She couldn't resist teasing him just a little bit.

"A Plan You-and-Me." He turned her in his arms and pointed her away from the window, in the direction of the couch in the center of the room. "Why don't you go have a seat? I think I heard Santa Claus on the roof earlier."

"Ross, it's the middle of the day. Santa doesn't come until it's dark. I may not have had much of a childhood, but I do know that."

"Just go sit on the sleigh...I mean, couch."

She did as she was told, wondering just what Ross had up his Santa sleeve. He walked out of the apartment without another word, leaving her very confused.

The time alone gave her a moment to reflect on the lowest point of her time after Hurricane Hope, when she'd discovered her estranged mother sitting on this very couch, buying items on credit cards she'd opened without Becca's knowledge or consent. Becca had felt so sick to her stomach when she realized her mother had only wanted to rekindle their relationship because of her perceptions of Becca's finances. After she'd kicked her mother out, Becca hadn't been able to look at this couch or the apartment for days.

But now, the room was full of sparkle and cheer and love. A tall spruce stood in the corner, decked with lights and colorful antique glass globes from Bretton's on the Boardwalk, a store in the historic downtown district that was dedicated to Christmas. Stockings were hung—albeit from the edge of the bar-top counter that swooped around the front of the kitchen. If she closed her eyes and took in a deep breath, Becca figured she'd almost be able to imagine the smell of chestnuts roasting on an open fire.

The sound of dog claws tap-tap-tapping on the hardwood floor broke up her festive daydream. Cookie walked in, his usual drooly tennis ball replaced with a fresh one that had been tied up with a red bow.

Behind him walked another Labrador retriever, this one sporting fur in a deep velvety-brown hue. A large red bow was tied around the dog's neck in lieu of a collar.

"Cookie, who's your friend?"

Becca didn't see Ross anywhere, and Cookie wasn't making proper introductions.

Cookie and the chocolate Lab sat by the couch, one on either side of Becca's feet. As they settled, Becca noticed a big white tag affixed with a narrow ribbon to the chocolate Lab's large bow collar. Intrigued, Becca leaned in and saw a message in small, neat handwriting.

My name is Cocoa. I've come all the way from Afghanistan to ask if you'll be my mama.

"Oh, Cocoa!" Becca swooped down and gave the big girl a hug. "Of course I will be!"

"She has one more question." Ross stood in the doorway, leaning casually against the jamb. His hands were balled up inside the pockets of his wide-wale corduroy pants. "You need to turn the tag over."

She couldn't figure out what the three of them were up to. With a slight tremble in her fingers, she reached out and tugged the tag upward. Tied to the top of the tag was a platinum band with a clear teardrop-shaped solitaire.

Will you marry me US? The tag had been carefully engraved.

Becca held the silver circle, staring at the words, unable to believe what had just happened.

"I've never known you to be much at a loss for words, Becca," Ross said evenly.

Becca took one short inhale, then another and another.

"I don't need a whole lot of words. Only one. The answer is yes."

Ross relaxed into a smile and snapped his fingers. Both dogs popped up and stood on their hind legs, giving a chorus of generous barks.

Love was found in moments like these. And it truly was the greatest gift she'd ever received.

You Don't Have to Leave Port Provident!
Start The Doctor's Unexpected Family Now

The storm has moved on, but the residents of Port Provident are just beginning the rebuilding process. What comes next for this special town? Continue the Port Provident: Hurricane Hope series and find out.

THE DOCTOR'S UNEXPECTED FAMILY

He wants to change the world. She wants to save her hometown.
They might just save each other.

Dr. Pete Shipley is on a mission to save lives around the world. City
Councilwoman Angela Ruiz is a single parent fighting to hold together
her hometown after Hurricane Hope tears through Port Provident,
leaving destruction across the community she has sworn to serve.

Together, they team up to found The Grace Space, a community
gathering spot in the heart of Angela's district, where residents can get
food, household goods, and basic medical care in the aftermath of the
storm. It becomes a place where the community's spirit can heal--and a
place where Pete's care begins to heal Angela's stressed-out heart as
well.

When Pete's long-awaited appointment to an international medical
mission comes, will the doctor follow his lifelong dream and leave Port
Provident, The Grace Space, and Angela and her daughter--or will he
stay with the family he didn't expect to love and change the world
without leaving home?

WANT MORE OF PORT PROVIDENT?

CAN I ASK YOU FOR A SMALL FAVOR?

If you liked this story, I'd like to ask you to please leave a review. Help me spread the word about Port Provident on Amazon. Most major retailers depend on an algorithm to boost a book's visibility among readers browsing for new titles. Reviews play a major role in how those algorithms work.

I'd appreciate your help in letting other readers just like you know about *Shelter from the Storm*'s hope, heart, and happily-ever-after. It's not about the length of the review—even just a few words like "Good story—I enjoyed it" may seem simple, but can help other readers like you know this is a story worth picking up.

PORT PROVIDENT: HURRICANE HOPE SERIES

Read the Entire Port Provident: Hurricane Hope Series

Shelter from the Storm
The Doctor's Unexpected Family
His Texas Princess
Holiday of Hope

Love Hallmark movies? Pick up Kristen's book October Kiss, based on
the Hallmark movie viewers love! Available anywhere books are sold
—in paperback, digital, and audio!
October Kiss from Hallmark Publishing

ABOUT KRISTEN

Kristen Ethridge writes Sweet Escape Romance—stories with hope, heart and happily-ever-after—for Harlequin's Love Inspired line, Hallmark Publishing, and Laurel Lock Publishing. She's a Romance Writers of America Golden Heart Award nominee and both an Amazon Christian Fiction and Inspirational Romance #1 Best-Selling Author.

You can find Kristen in her native habitat—a Texas patio—where she's likely to be savoring the joy of a crispy taco, along with a glass of iced tea. Scents from her essential oil diffuser are also a must, since she's a certified aromatherapist. She's almost convinced her family that it's normal to talk to imaginary people, as long it goes in a book.

Find her online at http://www.kristenethridge.com and on Amazon and Bookbub. You can get a free story for signing up for her newsletter at https://www.subscribepage.com/kristenethridgenewsletter. You can also follow her adventures in writing at www.facebook.com/kristenethridgebooks.

www.kristenethridge.com
https://www.facebook.com/KristenEthridgeBooks
https://instagram.com/kristenethridge

Don't forget…if you love sweet escape romances, join Kristen's newsletter!

ACKNOWLEDGMENTS

The Port Provident Animal Shelter has its roots in the heroic work done by the Galveston Island Animal Shelter during the time of Hurricane Ike. To those who worked tirelessly to save animals and later relocate and build out a new shelter in order to help the furriest victims of Hurricane Ike find new forever homes, thank you.

To the staff and volunteers of the Central Texas SPCA and the Humane Society of Williamson County in Leander, Texas—thank you for introducing me to two poodles more than ten years ago. Claire and Pierre have been blessings to me for more than a decade. There were clearly a lot of stray apricot poodles in town at the time, but I'm glad I got to be the mama to these two furry messes.

～

And as always, to my wonderful family: Brian, Carrie and Linnie…and 3.0, plus the adopted member of our family, Courtney. I set some crazy goals this year for my writing. While I'm the one who has to sit in the chair and put the words on the page, I couldn't do it without all of you. Muah.

"A righteous man has regard for the life of his animal…"
—PROVERBS 12:10

∼

Book Layout ©2013 BookDesignTemplates.com

CPSIA information can be obtained
at www.ICGtesting.com
Printed in the USA
BVHW071621110121
597448BV00003BB/195